THE FORBIDDEN CITY

MARY E. TWOMEY

MARY E. TWOMEY, LLC

THE FORBIDDEN CITY

Book Four in The Last Deadblood Series

By

Mary E. Twomey

COPYRIGHT

DEDICATION

For Jason.

Who fought for my family and never winced at the battle scars.

When the city she loves threatens to destroy itself in her absence, Colette knows she will have to return to the fight.

Hiding in the woods seemed like the only option when threats of abduction could not be ignored any longer. But when the vampire mating bond begins to take unfortunate turns, Colette isn't sure she will survive the changes.

The only way to cure her is for Rome to come back and fix the bond he broke. But if he cannot forget his affection for Colette, their forbidden love just might be the thing that tears the city apart.

"The Forbidden City" is filled with political intrigue and scandalous secrets, written by USA Today bestselling fantasy romance author, Mary E. Twomey.

MY DEAREST LOVE

I didn't pack a brush. In my haste to get somewhere safe, I didn't remember to pack a hairbrush. I guess I was more focused on escaping the city after Nico—my childhood best friend—publicly spat on me, then kicked and punched my face until it was black and blue.

At least I have a toothbrush, so there's that silver lining.

Actually, Orlando did the packing for me, but I try not to blame him for anything that was forgotten. He got me safely out of Mayfield, which was the right call.

Of all the twists and turns I anticipated when I moved back to Mayfield, intent on opening up a business that served both vampires and humans in Midtown, ending up in this rickety old cabin in the middle of the woods outside the city proper wasn't in the plan. Though I don't disagree with Orlando's insistence that I relocate here temporarily until Nino-Bear can be sorted out, this whole situation is less than ideal.

Not Nino-Bear. Nico. Nico Valentino is the man who beat me up. Nino-Bear is the mischievous boy I used to make mud pies with, back when life was simple and loving people was easy.

Nino-Bear doesn't exist anymore.

What a coincidence; neither does the girl in pigtails who used to make him laugh when he grew afraid of the big men with guns.

Though, as he is now one of the big men with guns, I imagine he has fewer things of which to be afraid.

Not me. I have plenty to fear, not the least of which are the spiders in this pre-war cabin in the middle of nowhere. Certainly this is a place a girl goes to be murdered and never heard from again. My cell phone doesn't have reception, though perhaps this is a good thing. I don't want to hear what the people of Mayfield are saying.

I'm sure the lie of me taking up with a vampire is well circulated by now.

It wouldn't have been a lie two months ago, yet here we are.

I wanted to be my mother—to pick up her mantle of being a vampire rights activist and lead the way for not just tolerance but acceptance of those different than us. She met with dignitaries and important policymakers, weighing in on issues with the gravity of someone who had been elected as a public servant.

Funny that nature selected her to be a weapon.

She was the Last Deadblood until she had me, and now I am the final weapon. My blood can be used to kill vampires, who generally live far sturdier lives than humans. But I don't want to be a beacon for war. I love the Valentino family—the head family of the vampire people. Or at least I used to.

Now I'm not so sure.

Nico was supposed to pretend to be my boyfriend. It was a dreadful plan, to be sure, but when Governor Ingrid Mason stops by, you go along with whatever she says. What I wanted was for the education budget to be divided equally in Mayfield, so that the vampire children in the West End had the same quality of books, computers and education as the privileged human East End children. What I wanted was for the city's public works budget to be split evenly, as well. That shouldn't be so hard a feat to accomplish, but apparently, I picked a stubborn issue for my first one to tackle.

I wanted to be like my mother and affect change with an effortless smile so the world wouldn't be so grim.

I didn't realize how much effort goes into concocting an effortless smile.

It was an uphill battle with no hope of success until

Governor Mason promised to throw her weight behind the proposal if I did one thing.

I needed to pretend to be dating a member of the Valentino family.

If only she knew the head of the Valentinos had recently broken my heart and ran off with the thing. Had she asked a month earlier, I would have proudly come out as dating the handsomest, noblest and most accomplished man I'd ever known.

Unfortunately, Mister Valentino turned out to be nothing short of ordinary. The moment things got too real for him, he split, ending what I thought was love without so much as a conversation.

It's just as well. I don't have time for silly things like love. I have history to change and minds to open. A pretend boyfriend is far better for the sort of life I lead.

I didn't expect it would be Orlando—the Valentino cousin who acts as their sentry.

I also didn't mean to mate with him. Though, to be fair, little is known about the vampiric mating bond. We're still learning the ropes as we go. For example, we learned that if I drink a little of Orlando's blood before bed in my evening tea, ailments that have taken a toll on my body for years seem to vanish. But if I miss a night, I am so cold by morning that not even the hottest bath can warm my skin.

Orlando gave me a flask of his blood to keep at the cabin while he's away dealing with Nico. He is also juggling the mess Mister Valentino left him in the West End when he split so abruptly. I'm to splash a few drops of Orlando's blood into my tea at night, giving Orlando a longer tether so he doesn't have to come back here every evening and risk leading a tail to the cabin who might want to abduct me.

It's laughable that anyone might believe the man a decade my senior, this family friend, might be the man I end up with. But for the sake of getting the education budget revisions passed sooner than next fall, I pray the world believes the staged photo of Orlando and I getting cozy in the backseat of his car is real.

I was in love with Orlando's cousin, but only Orlando, my brother, and his boyfriend know that.

My blood could kill Orlando. Still, the mirage of me dating a Valentino is what the governor requires, so that is the show we have given her.

Declan positioned the photo so Orlando's face was obscured by our hands, leaving it uncertain which Valentino I am dating, since Rome and Orlando look so similar. But the gold ring all the Valentino men wear with the family crest was visible, so the people have all the ingredients needed to make a rumor truly grow wings and fly.

I am far removed from the internet or any living thing (other than the spiders), so I have no idea if anyone bought the lie or not.

Either way, I decide to occupy my time this evening scribbling in a notebook Orlando brought me.

He does that sometimes—brings me something I desperately long to have but never asked for. It's part of the mate bond. He knows me well, even if he doesn't mean to be paying attention.

I wanted a journal to keep myself company while I remain isolated, so the next day, he showed up with groceries, a few changes of clothes and a journal, even though I never mentioned I wanted one.

It's silly, really. And Orlando is the opposite of silly. But my pen drags across the unlined beige pages, writing a letter to Orlando to make him laugh, and also to share my madness with someone.

I start out the letter in grand fashion, pretending we are soulmates separated by fate's cruel hand. In my lonely life overseas before moving back to Mayfield, I dreamed of having a dearest love to whom I could write sappy sonnets.

Orlando will tolerate my goofiness.

'MY DEAREST LOVE,

I PINE FOR YOU DAILY, AS IS MY RITUAL. EVERYTHING REMINDS *me of you. For instance, a spider landed on my toothbrush this morning. I missed you so badly that I plucked off six of his legs and paraded him around, pretending he was you. I was so good at conjuring your likeness in my imagination that I only remembered the spider was not you when I was kissing the hairy pest, and he up and died in lieu of returning my affections.*

How I pine for your songs.

I SNICKER AT THE IDEA OF ORLANDO SINGING AT ALL. I CAN barely believe I've seen him smile.

WHEN YOU SING OF MY BEAUTY, IT MAKES MY BREASTS GROW *three sizes. They rise to your song like unrequited mountains. Sing to me, my love. For without your melody, I fear my melons might shrivel up to mere raisins, and my soul shall in turn wither. For you are the sun, the stars and the entire solar system, while I am but a helpless, demure flower.*

Pluck me, my dearest love. My big sweetie pie.

-COLETTE

I READ IT AGAIN, LAUGHING AT MY PROSE. I PLAN ON READING this to Orlando in grand fashion in a lilting voice with plenty of theatrics.

If he ever comes back here. If he doesn't, I might die in the woods without anyone knowing where I've gone.

No, no. I shake that thought away because it simply isn't true. Declan knows where I am. He won't let me disappear, and neither will Orlando.

I haven't seen anyone in four days, though. Orlando brought me more than enough food to last the week, but after that...

I'm sure he'll come back any minute now.

Any minute now.

2

NO BLOOD, NO FOOD

It's been fourteen days since I have seen Orlando. I've gone over the budget for Mayfield and all the bylaws, making a list of which ones need to go if the world is to spin on its axis correctly. I have been savoring a sip of his blood each night before bed, but yesterday I drank the last drop, licking the tip of the flask clean as best I could.

I don't want to be dependent on anything, but I've learned years ago that some things simply cannot be helped. Though, to have Orlando's blood along with my medication was a welcome relief. It felt like I was cheating the system by some fateful twist of magic.

Only it wasn't fateful. It was dreadful, because I have run out of my meds *and* Orlando's blood.

I know things are about to get a whole lot worse.

I have only ever missed Orlando in the way one does

childhood friends they look back on fondly. But when the night drags on and I am no closer to sleep, my mind wanders to him more than it should.

Is he okay? He said he would be back days ago. A week ago.

I'm losing track.

But he left more blood for me than a few days' worth, so he must have known something might go wrong.

Is Orlando lying in a ditch somewhere? Surely I would feel something—some mystical snapping of the tether that ties me to his formidable presence.

It's cold in here. Ever since the sun set, I haven't been able to shake the chill that feels like ice running through my veins.

It is winter outside, though not terribly so. The dusting of snow adds a drafty chill to the cabin, but the heater does its job for the most part.

It's me who is cold, regardless of the weather. I am freezing in my bones. I know that it will only get worse, now that I have run out of Orlando's blood.

I sleep in fits and starts, waking often to check the windows for signs of Orlando's car. My dreams are haunted. There is no shape or reason to them, only an agony that echoes through my being. I scream Orlando's name over and over, but when I say it, the word mutates and sounds like I am shouting Ro... Mister Valentino's name. No matter how hard I try to call for Orlando, it is his cousin's name that belts out of me in the cavernous darkness of my nightmare.

When morning comes, I am no more rested than I was before the sun set.

I write more of my silly fake love notes to Orlando, but by the time night falls again, tears have splashed over the ink. My joints ache, which is no real surprise. My body wasn't built to last all that long. My mother only lasted until she was thirty years old. Factoring in my condition's unpleasant interruptions throughout my life, it is no wonder everything hurts before its time.

I should have five years left to live before my body gives up the good fight, but tonight, I worry that timeline I clung to is growing increasingly short.

And I had hopes that Orlando's blood would negate the doom of my genetics. But our vampire mate bond does me no good if he is nowhere near.

When I crawl into the bed, my stomach growls, reminding me that the empty cupboards are a problem all their own. I need Orlando's blood. No matter how badly I want to resist this whole idea, there is no lying to my threadbare joint fluid or the trembling of my limbs.

Tears fall without dignity or shame now. I clutch my pillow as the same awful nightmare overtakes me. I am bathed in darkness, unable to call out the right name. Every time I scream for Orlando, his cousin's name is on my lips.

I don't want to be scared. I don't want to be in pain. I don't want any of this.

Yet here I am.

When the sun rises, my limbs move as if I have been stored in an ice block. Everything is rigid, even as my body quakes uncontrollably. Even if there was food, I would not be able to feed myself. I can't grip much of anything without dropping or ripping it.

If this gets much worse, I will have a seizure, and that could be it for me.

I know I have to find Orlando. My phone doesn't work in this cabin, though, so I shower as best I can with my limited mobility, putting on my shoes with fingers that cannot maneuver the laces.

Anger rages in my breast. The physical therapist warned me not to wear shoes with laces. She warned me not to go into an occupation where dexterity was a necessity, too. Come to think of it, I've been warned off a whole lot in life, but that's only fueled my stubbornness.

I will not be twenty-five and unable to tie my own shoes.

I took my last pill a few days ago when I probably didn't even need it, because I had Orlando's blood in me. Now I've gone cold turkey off both, and my body is rebelling.

I scream at my shoe and throw it across the cabin, still unsatisfied when it smacks against the far wall. The wall should splinter and crack under the weight of my assault, but my shoe doesn't even leave a scuff mark.

For all my energy, I affect nothing.

The West End is still abandoned to ruin. Mayfield still runs rampant with bigotry. The world still views vampires as less than worthy of time and kindness.

For all my effort, I am an untie-able shoe, uselessly sitting in the middle of the woods.

I will die here, and only Declan will know where to find my corpse. Surely if Orlando was still alive, he would have come for me by now.

It figures my father would turn over a new leaf right before I die. He was dismissive, distant and surly my whole life, but in the past few months, he's been thoughtful—which is something I never thought I would be able to say about the sheriff.

I stare at my quaking hands, terrified because I cannot clench my fists anymore.

I won't be able to operate my phone if this keeps up.

Barefoot it is.

I do my best to be careful not to step on anything sharp as I walk out into the fresh woodsy air, but I soon realize that is easier said than done. I have lost all sensation in my feet—whether from the cold I cannot shake or from the curse of being the Last Deadblood, I cannot tell. The snow is only a dusting, but I need shoes to get through this without risking frostbite.

My phone still has no reception, even when the trees swallow the cabin behind me.

I cannot turn back until I call my brother. Until I call Orlando. Until I call anyone who might get me out of this mess of a life I cannot seem to escape.

I am wearing two pairs of pants, a t-shirt, a sweater and a jacket, but I am still shivering. My socks are soaked through with the morning frost and a quarter inch of snow. I lean on the nearest tree when my balance is questionable, but there is no amount of attempting to steady myself that actually does the job.

Still no reception.

Maybe this is Orlando's plan. It's a good one, to be sure. My big sweetie pie would have come for me by now if he didn't want me to die in the woods. He is more educated on vampire mating than I am. He knows I cannot be without his blood for more than a day or so. He is the one who told me as much.

My stomach tightens and then sinks when a horrible thought dawns on me: Orlando left me here to solve the problem of the world harboring the Last Deadblood. He doesn't have the stomach to stab me and end it all quickly, so he has left me here to die.

I could twist the charm on the necklace that Mister Valentino gave me. Orlando put it in my overnight bag in case there was an emergency. It's a trigger that sends my ex-boyfriend my location and tells him I am in danger. I could send the signal now, but I won't.

I don't wear that necklace anymore, because I would rather death swallow me than bear the pain of needing him to rescue me, and knowing he cannot be bothered. I couldn't call him right now if I wanted to, which I don't.

I wish that necklace meant a damn thing, but it doesn't. It's a broken promise that I will never forgive myself for believing.

I knew I would die alone, but I thought that meant I would die without a man in my life. I didn't realize it meant I would die with no one around for miles.

Without my brother.

Without sufficient mobility.

I am devolving into a shivering, sobbing mess of a human as I hurtle toward the end.

I wonder if I told Declan I loved him enough times. I wonder if he knows how proud of him I've always been.

I wonder if my mother will know who I am when I cross over to the other side of this life. Will she recognize me because we are the same, or will we be strangers to each other, adrift in our separate misery? She died giving birth to me. Maybe she won't recognize me, and even in this next life, we will be lost to each other.

I walk until my trembling legs go numb and give out. Then I crawl towards what I think is the edge of the woods, though there is no end of the trees in sight.

My tears wet the ground, thanking this life for the good things it gave me, and the missed opportunities that tried to garner my attention. I cry until I have no energy left.

I cannot lift my head. My limbs shake until the jerks become violent, making it harder to breathe.

I cry out into the empty forest, calling for someone to help me, for it not to end like this. I beg for help, but my plea comes back empty.

The world goes dark, swallowing me in its void as I prepare myself to die alone.

3

CARRIED AND CARING

It's been a while since I've been cradled. In fact, I think the last time was Daddy Valentino, carrying me inside when I'd fallen asleep under one of his enormous trees in the backyard. Of course, maybe it was a regular-sized tree, and I was just too small to see the world as it was. Everything seemed bigger when I was a little girl. Daddy Valentino seemed over the top with jovial love and affection when it was just our families, but then when I would catch clips of him on the news, his goofy laugh was nowhere in sight.

I miss being loved by a father figure. The sheriff wasn't the cuddly type. After I was sent away, Daddy Valentino and I never saw each other again.

I remember everything hurting mere minutes ago. Or was it hours? Days? My limbs are limp, my head lolling over an arm that trembles with every foot I am moved. My eyelids are too heavy to open, so I give up any semblance of fight. If my heart is beating, so be it. If it is not, and I am being transported into the afterlife, so much the better for the entire world.

I bring out the worst in people, though I don't mean to. I bring out fear in vampires. Even if I show up with a hug and a smile, I make them afraid because of what my blood can do to them.

I bring out wickedness in my own people. When they look at my face, more often than not, they see an opportunity for cruelty.

If I am in the arms of an angel right now, I do not know if they are taking me to a peaceful resting place or to undying torment.

I am certain I don't deserve either.

Though, I don't think an angel would be breathing this hard, struggling to carry me.

The creak of a door tells me we aren't in Heaven or Hell, but back in the musty cabin. With a grunt from my rescuer, I am lain on the couch with my champion kneeling on the floor beside me. "It's not enough. Coco, tell me I'm not too late."

Orlando's voice sinks into my psyche, comforting the frightened parts of me.

"You need more blood. Here." Orlando pinches my cheeks together, popping my mouth open. There's a hiss from him and then warmth that trickles across my tongue.

It's wrong to call this a flavor, because it's far more than that. Orlando's blood is more like a frame of mind, a peace that coats my insides and settles the unsteady parts of me.

My body curls around the source of sustenance I have been craving. My hands find sensation and purpose, reaching for his forearm so I can hold his wrist more securely to my mouth. My fingers don't work properly, so I paw at his arm to keep it close. My tongue laps at his cut, drawing as much of him into me as I can muster.

My eyes open as cognizance returns to my body like the trickling of the rain. I take in the inside of the unlit one-room cabin, and the silhouette of Orlando that is illuminated only by the moonlight shining in through the opened front door.

He's exhausted, poor thing. While I drink from him, I reach out and cup his cheek, letting him know that I am here, and I care about his wellbeing.

I've never drank directly from a person before. Orlando has always put his blood in a flask or a teacup for me to class it up.

I assumed drinking directly from him would make me feel feral, but it's not like that. His blood is the warm milk that calms my soul and nourishes my body.

Orlando didn't leave me to die. Whatever kept him from returning left welts and bruises across his face and arms.

I want to ask him what happened, but I can't stop drinking. I need this blood, this medicine, this antidote.

This friend.

I paw at his cheek.

"Easy," Orlando warns, his voice gravelly. Though I am sure he would never do this if there was light to shed on his actions, Orlando leans into my touch, allowing me to cradle his cheek while he catches his breath.

I lick his wrist several times while the wound begins to clot. "What happened?" I whisper, noting his shiver. "You were gone for so long."

Orlando pulls his arm away once I release it. His eyes close as he rocks from his knees to sit his butt on the floor. He rests his side against the couch and leans his head on me, resting his temple against my hip. "Rome left when he realized you weren't in Mayfield, so I've been doing most of the heavy lifting on my own. The West End needs Rome to come back for more than a few days. They sense he's gone, so they've started up all sorts of things they know he wouldn't allow. Makes the lessons I have to lay down that much harder."

Though Orlando and I have never been particularly physically affectionate toward each other, my hand finds its way to his hair. I like the weight of his head against my hip. It's a wonder I get to witness Orlando in any state of vulnerability or rest, so I cherish these rare moments.

His body relaxes against me. "I need to get back. I'll leave more blood before I go."

I let loose a derisive chortle. "I don't think so, Mister."

"I can't leave the city to its devices, Coco."

"For one night, you will. You're barely upright. You'll get yourself killed, going back into the city half-cocked like this. Then the West End will have no one." I sit up and slide off the couch to kneel beside him.

I love that my legs move freely and easily now. It's amazing what a little blood can do for my body.

Orlando grunts as he sits up more fully. "Why didn't you twist your necklace? I know you have it, even if you don't wear it anymore. I put it in your overnight bag. Rome would have come for you."

I scoff at the notion. "That's a wager I won't take. And thank you for the reminder, but I would sooner die than force your cousin to come back. I don't let people I don't respect see me when I'm vulnerable."

Orlando frowns at me. "Hey. He's scared, Coco. It's not as simple as normal boyfriend cold feet."

I keep my hand in his hair, twisting the black tresses and noting that he needs a touch-up around his temples. "Unfortunately, I don't give out prizes when men correctly identify an emotion. Scared is something we could have dealt with together. Scared is what I was when I couldn't breathe. He left me, Orlando. The greatest gift I can give is letting him be gone. I'm not touching that necklace."

Orlando winces when he tries to stand. "Ah!" He sits back down on the floor, holding his side.

Compassion swirls in me when I take in the scope of Orlando's injuries, though I am certain more are hiding beneath his bloodied suit. He is such a larger-than-life, unshakable figure in my mind. To see him breathless and worn rips at the optimism of the little girl inside of me. She took for granted that the men in her life would always be indestructible.

"Deep breaths," I tell Orlando as I unbutton his white dress shirt, which has puffs of red around his shoulder. I keep my eyes on his because I know he doesn't like unveiling any sort of weakness. "These clothes are coming off. You're going to take a shower so we can see what we're dealing with. If it's bad, I'm driving you to Declan while you sleep in the car."

"You can't go back to Mayfield yet," Orlando informs me, his expression torn between doling out a serious warning and withering into worry over his wounds being exposed. "I set Nico straight, but he's got followers. His crew isn't quite convinced that you existing is such a good idea." He winces when I work off his shirt and suit jacket. "And honestly, I'm not sure how sincere Nico ever is when he agrees to fall in line against his stubborn will. It's exactly as bad as I was afraid it would get. I brought you here to make sure none of that got anywhere near you. You're staying put until it's safe for you to come home."

I chew on my lower lip while I digest his warning. I cannot allow myself to dwell on my childhood friend's plot to destroy my business and run me out of town. There are more pressing things that must be dealt with first. Orlando is far more injured than I realized. My gasp fills the cabin as his bruised torso is uncovered.

I stand and turn on the cabin's overhead light, shutting out the moonlight as I bolt the door to stifle the wintry draft. "What did they do to my big sweetie pie?"

Orlando's upper lip curls in my direction, but I don't take offense. "Nothing. We sat down to tea and discussed that the humans who have ignored our needs are worth tolerating. They all agreed to practice patience while things change too slowly for even our grandchildren to notice."

My mouth pulls to the side. "When was the last time you ate anything?"

He shoots me an incredulous look. "That's all you're thinking about after what I just said?"

I cross my arms. "You're crabbier than usual. I'm willing to bet you haven't eaten in a while. I'm guessing you were too busy being a punching bag to stop for any real food."

Orlando harrumphs, but the motion makes him grab at his side. "I'm fine. Vampires heal faster than humans. These bruises won't be as bad by morning. You're worrying over nothing."

My tone turns to ice as I look down on him. "You are not nothing."

He rolls his eyes. "You know what I mean."

"And you know I'm not going to let you leave until you are back on your feet."

Orlando chuckles, though there's no joy in the sound. "That might work on Rome, but it doesn't affect me."

I wince at mention of my ex's name. "I really don't care what affects you. You're barely upright, so I'm in charge." I dig into his suit pocket and swipe his keys. "You have however long it takes for me to pick up some food and bring it back here for you to be showered and in bed. I mean it."

Orlando sighs, as if I am the one being exasperating. "You're wearing pajamas and you have bare feet. I took off your socks because they were icy and wet. You can't go out like that. And when exactly was the last time *you* showered and ate? You've thinned out. What's your excuse?" The second his words come out, his eyes widen. "Oh, Coco. You ran out of food, didn't you. I was gone too long. I only thought about you needing to drink my blood. I forgot about the fact that you probably didn't have enough actual food left."

A gentle smile sweeps over my face. "It's fine, Orlando. You've got a lot on your plate. I'll go out and get us something." Instead of moving toward the door, I bend down to help him stand. Each of his grunts wound me, making me wish I could call for justice on each of Orlando's attackers. "Who did this? Who would dare lay a hand on a Valentino?"

His breath fans over my face because I don't want to let him go. I'm afraid he might wobble on his feet. "I'm the off-brand Valentino, and you know it." Though, he doesn't say this with any sort of resentment. "I am Joseph Valentino's nephew, not his son. I'm the enforcer. This is what that looks like when the head of the family isn't there to command respect. I have to fight for it."

My eyes close as I attempt to rein in my temper. "Names, Orlando. Who did this?"

He rattles off a list of guys. "Are all of those Nico's people? Because it sounds like it."

"Yeah. Nico is a hothead. He didn't like the idea of having to pretend to be dating you. I'm not sure he has calmed down about it yet. But he will. He always does."

I am not so sure. "He calms down because his older brother is in charge. He has to obey the head of the family. I think Nico is testing the waters to see if he has to obey you."

Orlando lowers his head. "I know."

It's not often I witness Orlando like this. He is always in his work-mode, pressed and ready to go. Even after a fight, he somehow still appears ready for the next meeting—stoic and unscathed. But tonight, the bare bulb overhead shines down on his battered body, proclaiming to the whole of the rustic cabin that Orlando is a person capable of breaking, just like the rest of us.

It's not natural, but part of me feels it is necessary. Orlando isn't a hugger, but this state of despair warrants basic decency. I am careful as my cheek rests on Orlando's bare, barreled chest, my hand climbing up to rest over his heart. I suck in a stuttering breath when he stiffens. I know Orlando is unused to people being in his body space unless it's an assault, or unless it's Rome. I can tell by the stiffness in his torso that he doesn't know what to do.

I make the choice for us both. I reach down and link my littlest finger through his, prying my cheek from his chest. "Is this better?"

Orlando swallows hard. "I think so." He closes his eyes and lowers his chin. His expression comes across as guarded, and on the edge of a display of vulnerability he cannot tolerate. "We have to be careful. The mating bond is stronger than logic. You're going to want to be nice to me. You're going to want to stay close. That's not love, though. It's biology."

I take my time digesting his warning before I tilt my head up at him. "You really think I don't love you? Long before the mating stuff went down, did you not know how much I care about you?"

Orlando shoots me a dubious look. "Knock it off. I read that silly fake love note you wrote in your journal to me. If anyone saw that and didn't understand your warped sense of humor, we could have a real mess on our hands."

I don't let him brush off my adoration of all he is to me. "You saved my life, Orlando. You pushed me on the swings. You read to me. You fixed my doll when the arm kept falling off."

He glances around as if he is afraid the cabin walls might overhear and spill the secret that Orlando has always had a heart.

He's just very good at hiding it from plain view.

"Well, your doll was stupid. No matter how many times I fixed it, the arm kept falling off. And you were spoiled. You refused to pump your legs on the swing because you wanted to be pushed until you were an old woman." His little finger coils more firmly around mine, his bare chest broadening. "And you knew that bedtime book backwards and forwards. You didn't need me to read it to you."

"But I wanted you to. I like having you around. Always have." I motion between us. "This mate bond just means I get to say it all out loud without you squirming away as if someone looking up to you is weird and wrong."

Orlando's nose scrunches. He holds up our linked fingers. "That's what this is? You look up to me?"

I shoot him a look of disbelief. "Obviously. Who wouldn't?"

"Um, most people. A human looking up to a vampire is ridiculous. That's not how the world works."

I chuckle at his discomfort. "Of course I look up to you. You're always in control of your emotions. You command a room without saying a word." Hurt shines in my voice, though I don't mean for it to. "No one would dare abduct you."

Orlando hooks his finger under my chin, looking into my eyes as if commanding my very soul to surface from its hiding place. "Hey. No one is going to come after you if I'm around."

Though I've just praised him for controlling his emotions so well, mine have no such fortitude. Tears sparkle in my eyes as anxiety births from my lips. "I thought the reason you didn't come back was because you brought me here to die, but you didn't have the guts to kill me quickly. I thought you... you knew that... you knew that it would be easier if the Last Deadblood died, so people wouldn't have to deal with my blood."

Orlando snorts airily, his brows bunching together as if he is perplexed I would ever come to that conclusion. "People will always find something to fight over. They'll find reasons to be afraid and to bring fear to others. The fact that it happens to be you right now doesn't mean that eliminating you would get rid of the hate. They would just find another symbol to fight over." He shakes his head. "I'm sorry I took so long to come back here. I'm new to having a mate, and this is no ordinary pairing. I might be in over my head."

I can tell he didn't mean to admit that last part aloud. His eyes widen, so it's my turn to comfort him.

"How can I make it better?"

Orlando studies our linked fingers. "I'm not sure. I've never had anyone but Rome or my mother care if I eat. Care if I come home torn up. You might have to be patient with me. I don't know what to do when someone cares."

His words break my already fragile heart. I lean my cheek against his bare chest once more. His body is warm when I am cold. "You matter, Orlando. I've always cared about you. But maybe this is the first time you're hearing it." I bring his fist to my lips and kiss his little finger. "You're going to take a shower and lay down in the bed, okay? I'm going to get us some food. By the time I get back, you'll be feeling that much better."

I make to drop his hand, but he doesn't release his grip. When he speaks, his voice is quiet. "Don't let me get confused, okay? You belong to Rome, not to me."

I bristle at his phrasing, but I am not in the mood to argue the obvious fact that I only belong to myself. "I can do that." I touch my thumb to his. "I'm your friend. Your sister. And right now, I'm your warden. Shower and bed, old man. That's an order."

The corner of Orlando's mouth lifts. "Thanks for making a joke. Don't use your bank cards to buy anything, okay? Under the radar means no one can trace you. There's plenty of cash in the glovebox, along with a gun, should you need it." He shakes his head. "Never mind. I'll do it. What are you hungry for? I'll pick it up."

"I'm hungry for everything, and you're kidding if you think I'll let you go back out when you're halfway upright. It's not exactly under the radar for you to go around looking like an extra in a horror movie."

"Fine, fine."

I link my finger to his once more. "Orlando, it's okay to let someone take care of you."

His mouth firms. "No, it's not."

I ignore his pride because it won't do either of us a lick of good. I slide on my shoes and pull on my coat, taking his keys so he stays put for one whole night, where I can watch over him and make sure he doesn't fall to ruin.

My affection for Orlando shifts to something deeper, tethering my heart to his in a way I know I cannot sever. While it's nothing like what I felt for Rome, the familial tie I have to Orlando coils itself around my heart, holding me to him as I step out into the frosty night.

Yes, this is going to get complicated.

4

ORLANDO MY LOVE

$\mathcal{I}$t takes me longer than I expect to locate a fast-food restaurant that doesn't turn my stomach.

It is no surprise to me that Orlando keeps his car immaculately clean. Even a speck of dust wouldn't dare besmirch his dashboard.

I would have thought any food would suffice, given how long it's been since I have eaten, but apparently my stomach is only in the mood for quality meat, preferably rare.

Yes, I am well aware that I am a spoiled princess.

I have few plans to change that fact about myself.

Instead of something that comes out of a clown's mouth, I opt for waiting in the parking lot of a Mexican restaurant while they prepare what I am sure they assume is an order for a party of ten. When Orlando leaves again, I don't know when he will be back. I can't risk running out of food this time.

This time.

How long is this going to last? How long can Orlando possibly keep this up? He needs help controlling the upset that Nico has drummed up, but Mister Valentino is nowhere in sight. Plus, part of the deal the governor made us was that I had to pretend to be in a public relationship with one of the Valentinos. It's hard to do that when we are in hiding. While I am certain the picture Declan posted of Orlando and I looking all together and scandalous has bought us some time, at some point we need to go back to Mayfield and give the people a real show.

Then we get fair and equal education for the children in the West End. We get money from the city to fix up the West End.

Funny how politics work.

Once Orlando is back on his feet, I will go with him.

My stomach sinks as I pick up the food and start driving back to the cabin. Even with me by Orlando's side, the West End won't fall in line. They need the man who can face them all with the fierce determination that they can and shall rise above the poor lot they've been dealt in life.

They need the man who is afraid of nothing, except being with me.

I need to call Mister Valentino home, or Orlando is fighting a losing battle.

While I would rather go blind than see Mister Valentino's face again, I am starting to learn that I would gladly crawl through broken glass if it meant Orlando might be granted a better life.

Orlando is taping up his wounds when I come inside with far too much food. I ordered it all before I realized we wouldn't be staying here all that long. Maybe a day or two, until he heals up.

Then we can return home so the people see that Orlando isn't a goon who can be pushed aside with brute force.

I frown at his grunting as he tries to stretch the bandage tape across his side in the doorway of the bathroom. "Let me do that. Hold on." I set the food on the table and move to the corner of the living room area to reach for my overnight bag. I like that I have to dig for the necklace, that it has been discarded to the bottom of the bag, where garbage goes to die.

Such a little thing. At the time it meant so much, but now it's a mere tool.

Just like me.

I suppress the angst that threatens to rise up and choke the bravery from my body. The hearts on the charm tangle together, making them look like they belong hooked around each other.

Not anymore.

Both thumbs press on the edges of the silver circle as I take a steadying breath. Once I do this, there is no going back.

"What are you doing?" Orlando asks, moving out of the bathroom's open door to stand by my side.

"What has to be done." With a sharp inhale, I twist the two halves of the necklace. The alert will trigger Mister Valentino's matching necklace to vibrate, telling him that I am in danger.

It will also give him my location.

"Good. That's a relief." Orlando is shirtless and showered, wearing the trousers that have been stained with his own blood and I hope his enemy's. "Rome will come back and stay with you here. You'll see that he was just scared. Then everything will go back to the way it was."

I clasp the stupid trinket around my neck, wearing it like a sign that reads "for sale". "I called him to come back for you, not for me. You can't do this alone." My eyes avoid his because I worry I have become a shell of a person who used to have purpose. "It's time to go home. Once you're back on your feet, I will drive us to Mayfield. I'll go back to my salon and Mister Valentino will help you get the West End in order again. He can keep Nico in line."

Orlando shakes his head. "No. Rome shouldn't come back to Mayfield unless that's where he wants to be. He will stay here with you."

I straighten as I move to the cupboard to pull down two cups for us. "Your words are honorable, but I won't let you die because of them. Mayfield needs Mister Valentino, so he will do his duty, just like you and just like me."

Orlando's jaw tightens. "His choice needs to be his own."

"Why? Our steps were determined before we could walk them ourselves. You were raised to be Mister Valentino's right hand. I was born to be the bomb walking about, waiting for the world to either be calm enough so I don't detonate or perhaps hurl me at the other side to level their enemy." I lift my chin. "Mister Valentino will do his duty by his people. I don't care how his heart shrivels and dies because of it."

My words are cold and unfeeling, but they suit me perfectly. I have no pity with which to cradle a grown man who ran out on me seconds after I was suffocating.

In fact, my soul has very little sensation at all anymore.

Orlando lowers his chin. "You cannot possibly be this cold."

"Actually, that's the only thing I can be, Orlando my love. I tried having a heart, but it didn't matter. When I sold myself with this charade of us dating to help give Mayfield a brighter future, that's when I did my duty for your people. In public, you are Orlando my love." I fill the old cups with water from the tap. "In private, you are Orlando who leaves me be."

He grunts as he sits down at the rickety table. "This is just sad, Coco. This isn't how you were supposed to turn out. You were the last hope for us all. If you had a heart, it didn't matter that none of us did. You were supposed to survive everything and find a way to show the world that Mayfield didn't break you."

I raise my nose in the air. "I am not broken. I'm getting things done. This is my role. I am finally finished being young and foolish. I can step into my birthright now with nothing slowing me down."

Though Orlando's stomach growls, he stares at me as if searching for something familiar in the mask I am wearing. The mask fits me far better than my own distorted, sad face ever did. "I don't like this," Orlando rules, finally reaching for the nearest takeout box. "But whatever gets the two of you back together, I guess."

I take the box from his hands and give him a different one. "That has fish tacos. You won't like that. You want rare meat." I hand him his water. "And your cousin and I are never getting back together, much to his immense relief, I would guess. If he cares if I am dead or not, he will come back and be assigned to you."

Orlando snorts, taking the plastic fork and spearing his steak enchilada. "You're giving orders now, are you?"

I don't answer because I am surprised to find that is exactly what I am doing, whether I have earned that authority or not.

No matter. It's the right call, and I am not afraid to make it.

I squeeze the lime wedge over my fish tacos and drizzle cilantro dressing over top. Though it smells wonderful, my stomach longs for rare red meat. I frown because my brain knows the fish taco is what I usually would prefer.

What is wrong with me?

I thought I was craving rare red meat because Orlando wanted it, but now that he is eating it, I am ravenous for his meal.

Orlando's brows pinch together. "Have some of my enchiladas," he insists, cutting one of the wet burritos in half. He sniffs the fish tacos. "They smell fine. I don't know why, but I need you to have half." He shrugs because that is the least perplexing element of the evening.

I lower my chin, ashamed of myself for subconsciously making him give up part of his meal that I know he wants. "I was just thinking I was starving for rare red meat. I'm sorry. I didn't mean to make you give up half your dinner."

Orlando waves off my apology. "You didn't say a thing. It's the mate bond. You need more red meat, so I won't be able to calm down until you get it."

My nose crinkles. "This is dysfunctional."

Orlando shovels food into his mouth as if he cannot be bothered to care if something is emotionally or mentally healthy. It's a problem, so he fixes it. Nothing more complicated than that to him, I guess.

He keeps his eyes on his food while he talks. "The less you question it, the easier life will be. If I hadn't questioned why I needed you to have some of the enchiladas, you would have had it a minute earlier."

I square my shoulders, determined to get this right. "Mating is an uncommon occurrence, right?"

Orlando's head bobs. "I've only heard stories of couples who have bonded. Never met any myself. But every now and then someone will claim that their great-grandparents were mated or something like that. I never thought all that much about it, but now I would kill for some actual research on the subject. Honestly, I don't care about being upset that this is happening to us. Or maybe I can't care. Looking after you is nothing I didn't do growing up. Now I have a cheat sheet, is all."

My expression tightens but I loosen up when I realize the same thing applies to him. "And I get to look after you."

"Why do you think I'm not putting up all that much of a fight when you decided Rome would come back to help me? If the mate bond is telling you that's what I need, I might not like it, but I can't exactly argue with omniscience like that. The bond knows what I need, and it tells you. I have to start trusting it and get over my pride."

I let out an airy one-noted laugh through my nose. "Easier said than done."

He extends his fist to me and sticks out his littlest

finger. "We've both faced more complicated things than this. Maybe this is nature's way of cutting us both a break."

I link my pinky around his, softening at the cuteness. "I never thought of it like that." I motion with my free hand between the two of us. "It didn't occur to me that this could be a good thing. A blessing."

"Just because we're not romantically involved doesn't mean we can't milk this for all it's worth. I, for one, plan on making sure you live to see the world change, because you deserve to see the fruits of all you've been fighting for." His eyes fix on his food. "I am determined that you will live longer than your mother. She didn't have me around. She didn't have my blood to combat her genetics."

My eyes moisten as the mask of stoicism slips off my face. "Do you really think so?"

Orlando tightens his hold on my littlest finger. "I know so. My blood is better than your medicine. The mating bond ensures that my body keeps yours healthy. You've been taking this whole changing the city thing at a run—partly because it needs it badly, and partly I know because you're five years away from the age your mother was when she died. Now that you're going to have longer to live, maybe there are more things we can tackle. And maybe we can breathe in between battles."

Orlando isn't a hugger, but if he was, this would be the moment for it.

A tear splashes atop my enchilada. "Thank you," I whisper, "Orlando my love."

Orlando snickers at the name I plan on using far and wide when we get back. "No problem, Colette my dove."

I don't know why that makes me laugh, but an uncouth sound bursts out of me when I picture people's reaction to Orlando calling any woman his dove. "Oh, that's perfect. I love it."

We grin without caveat while we demolish the enchiladas. Then we start in on the fish tacos, which my stomach tolerates more graciously now that I've got red meat in my gut.

My fingers are sticky, and my eyes lidded when we both declare a surrender to the feast.

I wash up while Orlando languidly puts the rest of the food away, his chest still bare.

"Bed," I order, pointing toward the sleeping area in the corner. It's a studio layout, so there aren't separate rooms for the bedroom and living room.

Orlando scoffs. "If you think I'm taking the bed, you're crazier than I thought you were when you opened that salon in Midtown. I found you on the forest floor, barely alive. To bed with you, Colette my dove."

The nickname isn't strictly necessary since we don't have an audience, but I lean towards it all the same. "Orlando my love, if you think I'm taking the bed when you are barely upright, you don't know how stubborn I can be. Plus, the mate bond demands *I* give *you* the bed. I won't be able to sleep even if you somehow manage to win this argument, because I'll be awake all night, worried about you."

Orlando chuckles, running his hand over his tired face. "Oh, fine. But that's not going to work next time."

I smirk at him. "Sure, it will."

Orlando is barefoot as he moves toward the bed. He glances over his shoulder a few times, checking my whereabouts as I wind down for the night. He places two blankets plus his comforter on the couch for me.

"You're doing it again," I remind him. "You can't keep taking care of me at the expense of taking care of yourself. You need a blanket, Orlando my love. It's winter outside."

I can tell he wants to argue, but the chill coming in through the old windows is on my side.

He takes back the comforter, but waits to lie down until he has legit tucked me in.

I smirk up at him. "I'm not five anymore, Orlando. You don't have to do this."

"Let me?" It's a request with just as much helplessness as boldness.

I pretend it doesn't affect me that he tucks the blankets around my body and makes sure my hair isn't strewn in my face, but the truth of the matter is that I didn't get a whole lot of tender paternal moments after Daddy Valentino passed.

I find comfort in the sound of Orlando's heavy breathing when he finally lies down. It's a toneless lullaby that cradles me as I drift off to sleep, hoping that the morning greets us with a better tomorrow.

5

MISTER VALENTINO

A hand on my cheek rouses me just enough to bat it away. "Knock it off, Declan."

"Mistaking me for your brother is a low blow, but I guess I deserved that."

Whatever dream I was having is long gone now. I jerk awake, recoiling from the touch I know all too well. "Huh?"

None other than Rome Valentino switches on the light, making me wince with discomfort and shield my eyes as I blink the world into view.

I thought I was prepared for the sight of him. I summoned him here, after all. I didn't expect him to get here so soon. "What time is it?"

When I slide my legs to the chilly floor of the cabin, Rome puts his hands up. "Slowly, tré-sur. Where are you hurt?"

My jaw stiffens at the term of endearment. "I'm fine. It's

your cousin you should be worried about." I jerk my thumb to the bed in the corner of the cabin. "Orlando's been taking the brunt of every jaded vampire's anger since you skipped town."

Rome's gaze darts from me to the bed, where I notice Orlando has stopped snoring. "You called me for Orlando?" He says it like that's the silliest concern anyone might have. "You and your bleeding heart."

"Try to sound a little more patronizing next time." It hurts to look on Rome's beautiful visage, so I try not to stare directly at him while I speak. "Orlando needs help because you abandoned him to look after the West End on his own. He was barely upright when he got here." I probably look a mess, my brunette curls doing whatever they feel like with no hope of a hairbrush, but I convince myself I don't care. What I look like doesn't matter because there is no one here I am trying to impress.

Still, I'd assumed Rome was farther away and would take more than half a night to get here.

Rome scoffs, looking over my shoulder to the bed. "Orlando, you alright?"

"Yup."

I roll my eyes and stand. "Honestly. I can't even with you right now. I'm sure Orlando will heal alright, but that's not the point."

I have never seen Rome unshaven or unkempt, but he certainly is both of those things tonight. His shirt is untucked and wrinkled. His hair is in desperate need of a trim, and is sticking up in the back.

I motion to Rome's form. "I don't care whatever midlife crisis you've found yourself in; you need to get yourself together and deal with your family. Handle the West End. Orlando's presence doesn't do as much to keep everyone in line as the two of you together. If he goes back by himself, he's bound to get himself killed."

I don't look directly at Rome. I use any excuse to avoid eye contact. I want to feel nothing, but it's harder when he is standing right in front of me, looking like a heartbreak ready to happen all over again.

Rome takes a step back, his hand rubbing his dark facial hair. "You didn't call me here to talk or because you were in trouble."

I rub a crick in my neck. "I'll pack up my things while the two of you catch up." I was going to wait until Orlando was more healed up before we left the cabin, but these are tight quarters, and I don't want to be near Rome a second longer than I have to.

Orlando brings himself to sit up on the bed. "Go wait in the car, Coco."

I don't argue because I don't want to be here for this conversation. The Valentino family business is, well, their business.

Apparently, ten seconds is all Orlando is willing to wait before he opens the can of worms.

Orlando stands while I search for the car keys. "How was your little vacation, Cousin?"

Whatever meekness sneaked itself into Rome's personality is gone now. He puffs his chest, his feet shoulder-width apart, chin raised. "It was sufficient. I'm back."

Orlando glowers at his cousin. "Glad to hear it." Orlando's upper lip curls. "Nico beat up Coco while you were off doing who knows what."

Rome whips his head toward the door just before I exit. "Nico did what?" The news sets off a stream of Rome's best symphony of cussing. I get the highlights before I close the door behind me.

I don't want Rome involved in that. At least, not near me. Let him deal with Nico back in Mayfield. I don't want to know a thing about any of it. I want to go home.

I unlock Orlando's car and slide into the backseat. Even shut inside the car, I can hear the incoherent yelling echoing through the woods.

The two of them are in the cabin for quite a while, and don't emerge for a good fifteen minutes. Rome's lip is bloody, but luckily the tinted windows keep my wide eyes from view. I don't want him to know I am concerned.

I'm not.

Nothing about his distress stirs my internal whimpering in the least.

That's what I force myself to believe, anyway.

Rome pauses outside my window, but I don't lower it,

nor do I open the door. I don't think he can see me through the tinted window or the moonlight, but his hand touches on the glass all the same. Rome stares into the car, his hard gaze seeming to penetrate through the barrier in an attempt to pierce the armor I keep firmly in place.

"I will fix this," he vows.

It's not a plea: Rome is too sure of himself for that. It's a promise I am meant to keep close to my heart to help me sleep at night.

The problem is that he left me, so trust is too big a leap for me to attempt.

When Orlando emerges, he's got my things and his, plus the food from the fridge. He sets them in the trunk and then slides into the front seat. "I didn't tell him," Orlando explains in a gust. He looked so controlled when he stalked out of the cabin, but as he backs out of the path and turns onto the main road, he doesn't bother posturing to convince me.

I'm grateful we don't have to pretend. This whole situation is troubling. If we can't be honest about that, it's never going to get any better.

I fiddle with the zipper on my jacket. "I wish he didn't need to know about our mating bond, but you two are close. There's no room for secrets in your family. Not one this big, anyway."

Even though that rule holds true for Orlando, if Nico

ever found out that Rome and I had been together, that hothead would never be able to cool down.

Orlando's jaw tightens. "I'll tell him once he deals with Nico."

I close my eyes and lean my head against the seat. "One disaster at a time."

Orlando and I are quiet while he drives. Once I am in cell phone range, I see that Declan has been blowing up my phone.

"What's going on?" I ask him when our call connects.

"Coco, thank goodness. Fintan lost his mind."

My stomach drops. My oldest brother's temper isn't exactly what most would call stable. "What happened?"

"Only the obvious. Fintan saw the media coverage and went ballistic. When he didn't find you at your house, I had to tell him that you were in hiding until the craziness blew over. Dad's upset, and you know how the two of them are. They feed off each other's anger."

"I'm on my way home now. Should be there by sunrise."

"Fintan's been hunting for Nico. Luckily the little punk's been smart enough not to show his face in Midtown after what he did to you, but it's bad."

"Why is Fintan like this?" The question isn't meant for Declan or Orlando to overhear, or really for anyone to have to actually grapple with to sort out an answer. "Fintan doesn't care about me. He never calls, never visits, but he jumps on the opportunity to defend the family honor if there's a promise of violence. It's so fake, the whole thing."

Declan doesn't argue. "I say for Christmas, we pitch in and buy him a punching bag. Maybe take him to Anger Management. Tell him there's a bad guy there he needs to keep an eye on."

I snort at Declan's suggestion. "Thanks for making a joke. I'm sorry. I know I'm being a pill. I just want this whole thing to go away."

"About that." The turn in Declan's tone has me narrowing my eyes.

"What's wrong?"

"Fintan saw the picture of you and Orlando looking all cozy. The sheriff flipped out. I had to tell them it was fake, or you know it would have gotten bad. The world thinks that picture is of you and Rome, but Fintan and the sheriff know it's Orlando because I told them that bit. Not the mate bonding, just about the fake show you two have to put on for the governor."

I nod. "That's fine. They can keep it quiet?"

"They get it. You're trying to fix the West End, so you're giving the world a good show in order to get your proposal passed. They think it's a..." I can tell my brother is fishing around for more polite words, "...a not great idea, but the train has already left the station, so they're going to keep the secret." Declan clears his throat. "But Dad wants to have a few words with Orlando."

I glance at the man in the driver's seat, wanting to shield him from my father's scrutiny. "That's not necessary."

Orlando keeps his eyes on the road, but I know he can hear the conversation well enough.

"I'm sure the sheriff will disagree. I'm just giving you a head's up."

I chew on my lower lip. "Thanks. How are you?"

Declan exhales. "Other than worrying myself sick, I'm good." Declan tells me he is going to stop by in a couple hours before he heads to work to help me get settled back in.

When the call ends, my body feels stiff from my lack of sensible slumber. I keep my eyes on my phone as I text Fintan a quick, "Stand down. The Valentinos are dealing with Nico." Then I put my phone in my purse, so I don't have to read whatever frustration my eldest brother spews my way.

"Is Fintan going to be a problem?" Orlando asks quietly.

Rome's car leads the way home, but I don't want to see it. I close my eyes and lay my head back, laughing joylessly to myself. "Fintan is never happy unless he is being a problem."

I don't expect comfort to come when I have to deal with my family, or when I have to deal with anything.

Declan and I have each other, so that's who I spill my heart out to. If Declan is not around, I'm on my own.

When Orlando reaches back to link his little finger around mine, a mix of angst and calm jostles around inside of me. He knows I am upset. My frustration must be palpable for him to have picked up on it.

I don't like being a person who needs comfort, but I don't let go of Orlando's finger until he pulls into my driveway.

I'm not sure I am ready to deal with the world just yet, but knowing that I won't have to hold my chin up by myself is a relief I don't take for granted.

6

COOL AND CALM CHAOS

One of my best skills (other than doing hair) is pretending. I put my best pleasant smile on when I go to the salon the next morning, unwilling to dignify the scandal of me taking up with a Valentino with anything other than a demure quirk of my lips. My personal life should be no one's business, but the whole point of Orlando and me getting together is to make our pairing everyone's business.

Oh, the joys of politics.

I love my stylists for many reasons, including that I only had to tell them the highlights this morning before the shop opened, and they were good to go.

Rachel has been incredible at handling the salon in my absence. Having a solid branch manager gives me the space to do all sorts of fancy things, like flee from a threat of abduction.

I am adequately seasoned when it comes to preparing my communication when I am about to go into battle. Rule number one: stick to the basics.

1. Yes, I am dating a Valentino. He is the love of my life. End of story.
2. Yes, everyone saw Nico beat on me, thanks to the video footage that's been circulating the internet. I forgive him and wish him well. The world is changing, and that is hard for people to accept. No further questions.

WHILE I'M DOING HAIR, REPORTERS FILTER INTO MY SALON and take up residence in my waiting area. They toss out question after question, but after my two talking points, I give them nothing other than a pleasant yet dismissive smile. I keep my focus on my clients as best I can, practically fighting to keep my eyes on the hair I am cutting. My client deserves my undivided focus, but the reporters are making it difficult today.

I do my utmost to set the tone for my salon, and eventually the reporters lose their gusto and trickle out.

Rachel casts me a look that silently asks if I am okay.

I reply with nothing other than a serene smile.

Of course I'm okay. If any reporter asks, I am wonderful.

When I finally close up for the night, the armor of appearing cool, calm and collected begins to shatter. I am tired, crabby and stiff, grateful the workday is over.

A to-do list scrolls through my head as I shut off the lights and move toward the exit. I need to print out the labels for the next order of shampoos and conditioners tonight and stick them on the filled bottles tomorrow. Then I need to drive the orders to the store and drop them off because shipping them to Dana's Greens and Grabs store would cost a ridiculous amount.

So engrossed in my mental list am I that I don't realize there are Valentinos in the parking lot until I am halfway to my car.

Startled, my hand flies to my chest. "You scared me!" flings out of my mouth before my brain registers just who it is I am staring at. My expression tightens when I take in none other than Rome standing outside his black sedan. "If you're in need of a haircut and a shave, you can come back during normal business hours. The salon is closed."

It's difficult to pretend that the sight of him doesn't jerk my heart around in my chest, but I have been pretending to be calm all day long. This is nothing different, though my armor is sufficiently heavy and worn.

Except that the way that Rome stares at me leaves no

room for lies. He sees straight through me, leaving me naked before him, despite the shield of indifference I try to keep on me at all times.

He is showered now, though his facial hair has grown in, casting a shadow across his chiseled jaw. His shirt is tucked in and unwrinkled, his demeanor that of Rome before he left me.

I am supposed to tell him about the bond between Orlando and myself, but this hardly seems the right setting. Though, truly, I am not sure what the right setting might be.

"You're walking to your car alone," he comments, his expression hard and disapproving.

"Well spotted. I also brushed my teeth all alone." I motion to the flood lights he had installed. "I have these. People are less likely to do evil things when there's light shed on their actions. Goodnight."

I turn back to my car, but Rome moves toward his trunk. "I've got something for you."

I cannot imagine what Rome could possibly have for me, but intrigue stills my departure. "I don't need..." But what Rome pulls from his trunk isn't something I expect in the least. A gasp steals my refusal when Rome lifts his brother out of the trunk and drops him onto the asphalt. "Nico!"

The youngest Valentino is bound and thoroughly

bruised. There was no gag used because Nico knows screaming for help isn't the way to get out of this.

Rome kneels behind his brother and cuts his bindings loose. "Tell Coletta what you've learned, Nico."

I snarl at Rome. "That's Madam Deadblood. What did you do?"

A flash of regret compromises Rome's cold demeanor, but he recovers his control quickly. "Apologies, Madam Deadblood. Nico stepped out of line while I was away. I merely matched a bruise for each one his men put on Orlando's body, plus the ones he put on you. I wanted you to see. If you are not satisfied, I will continue."

I know this is the way things are done, and sure, part of me feels mollified that Orlando's injuries are being held to account. However, this is not the way I wish to spend my evenings.

I should tell Rome I am satisfied and leave. I should go home and get into a hot bath so my muscles can relax. Though I am not near as bad off as I was before I started drinking Orlando's blood, I've still been on my feet all day, fending off reporters and catching up with Rachel to make sure things were in order during my absence. Plus, it's about time for more blood—an issue of which my body is well aware.

I want to go home.

But I know that this beating will not satisfy me.

"You denied me," I tell Rome, swallowing the bile in

my stomach as I stare down the Valentino brothers. "The punishment was mine to give."

Rome's brows raise. "Apologies, Madam Deadblood. Feel free to settle it now, then. Nico won't fight back."

Nico is on all fours, heaving like a beast through his teeth. He spits blood on the pavement, his head lowered in submission.

Good. Arrogance is a dangerous tool in Nico's hands.

I put my things in my car and make my way toward Nico, pretending as best I can that I am in perfect control of everything in my life. It feels powerful to tower over him, to know that I could kick him until he bleeds, and I wouldn't be out of line. Nico attacked me in my own workplace in front of my employees and my clients. He tried to start a war when what I was trying to do was help his people get a quality education and fix up their end of the city.

I could kick him in the head right now.

Part of me really wants to unleash my misery on this man.

"I can do anything I want to him?" I ask Rome.

Mister Valentino studies my stalwart expression. "Short of killing him, yes. He disrespected you."

My limbs are sore as I lower myself to my knees, resting my hands atop my thighs. My pink, short pencil skirt rides up, but I don't care. "Nico, look at me."

I wait because I know the effort is more than he wants

to give. Nico doesn't want to look at me and really see who I am. He wants me to be guilty and wrong, which I might very well be, but still I wait until his eyes meet mine, however guarded we both might be.

Nico is breathing hard, but his breath comes in short pants.

I can tell he's cracked a rib from the way his movements are limited on his left side.

"Listen to me, Nico," I say quietly. "I do not hate you. You are not worth hating." His upper lip curls, but I keep on. "Your anger is grief wrapped up in a pretty dress. I'm sorry my blood got Daddy Valentino killed, but from now on, *I* will be the only person who beats me up for that. I don't need to tell you that I had no control over any of it; you already know that. You are done throwing tantrums, understood? We are not children anymore."

Nico has blood drooling out of the corner of his mouth, yet he still manages to appear haughty. *Freaking Valentino.* "Understood."

My nostrils flare but my voice remains steady and quiet. "I am not finished. I have no interest in matching you blow for blow. I require you to take me out for coffee at the shop across the street just there. Once a week. We'll sit down for exactly half an hour and act pleasant with each other. You need to repair the damage you did between our families not just to me, but to the public. We need to be photographed not trying to murder each other."

Nico groans. "Can you just beat me up instead?"

"I also require a hug."

"You can't be serious."

Rome presses the bottom of his shoe to Nico's rear. "You'll do as she says."

Nico hangs his head. "How many outings?"

"Until I am satisfied the entire world believes we are the best of friends. I guess it depends on your acting skills. Your bruises are pretty, but they do nothing to clean up the mess you made. The world's problems are bigger than yours. It's time you understood that."

Rome nods, and I swear I see a glimmer of pride directed at me.

I don't care. I'm not doing this for him. I have my eye on the prize: equality for vampires and peace in Mayfield.

Screw Rome and screw his approval.

"Nico agrees to your terms," Rome replies.

Despite the fact that I am wearing a white blouse and pink skirt that I really don't want to get blood on, I scoot toward Nico, extending my arms. I don't smile, nor do I make a single effort to appear welcoming.

Nico crawls to me, cradling his side with a wince. At first, he stops short, no doubt expecting me to clear the remaining gap.

Nope. I'm not about to make this easier on him. In fact, when he raises up on his knees before me, I don't wrap my arms around him but instead wait for him to coil his arms around me.

That's right, jerk. You're going to hug me and hate it. Enjoy your life.

I haven't hugged Nico since I was a newly minted teenager. He doesn't smell the way I remember, and apparently, he has forgotten how to hug entirely—a lesson that can be relearned, I am sure.

I rest my head on his shoulder, squeezing my eyes tight because I want to bathe in this feeling. As if my heart wasn't already shattered. This moment, however forced, imprints itself on the inside of my soul—a place I didn't think Nico had access to anymore.

Before I release him, my vindictive nature flares up. I dig my hand into Nico's left side, putting pressure on his broken rib. He stiffens and bites back a scream, but I hold tight to the man who sent me to the hospital.

"You will not cross me again. Do not imagine I will not hold you accountable for every terrible thing you've put me through." I dig harder into his side, relishing his howl that finally births into the night. "You cannot possibly punish me more than I have already punished myself for your father's death. From now on, you will leave me to my self-loathing. I can manage that well enough without you."

When I release him with a shove, my insides are ready to rend themselves in two. My hands press to the silk stretched atop my thighs as I bow my head, praying for a better life than this.

The Valentino family will be my undoing. If Mayfield doesn't kill me, my demise will surely be the fault of these men I should never have loved.

Rome makes to help me to my feet, but I scowl at his offer. "You will not touch me again, Mister Valentino." When the formal address rolls out of me, I instantly love it. I don't have to say his name just because he is back in town. I don't even have to think it. We are nothing to each other now. I don't have to be haunted by his very presence. Though I am anything but graceful, I manage to make it to my feet. "In fact, if you see me bleeding out on the side of the road, I prefer you leave me to die."

Rome opens his mouth but shuts it again once he remembers our company. "Apologies, Youngblood."

"Madam Deadblood," I correct him with a snarl. "I will see Nico next week at the coffee shop. I trust he will be presentable before then?"

Rome inclines his head to me, his hair slightly disheveled in the back. "As you wish, Madam Deadblood."

"Good. Then there is no need to see your face after tonight. Nico is forgiven. You are well forgotten." I turn on my heel and walk to my car, putting distance between myself and the chaos they bring.

"Colette!" Rome calls after me. The sound is a

mourning cry that makes me lose my step, but still, I keep going.

I don't look back. I don't want him to see how badly he affects me.

In fact, I don't want him to see my face ever again.

7

ORLANDO'S DRY WINE

Orlando frowns at me when he walks in the front door, using his key to get in. "Shouldn't you be sleeping? It's two in the morning."

"Is it?" I know what time it is, but that doesn't affect whether or not I can go to sleep. "I'm just finishing up."

That's a lie, but it's one I keep telling myself.

Orlando doesn't call me on the fib, but instead goes about his nighttime routine. Now that Rome is back, Orlando is patrolling the streets again, kicking down the doors of halluci-dens until odd hours of the morning.

He takes his shoes off and then heads for the shower, washing the blood off his hands, though it always manages to come back.

I take a short break to heat up his dinner, pouring him a glass of tempranillo because on my way home, that mysterious tug in my gut told me I *needed* to buy a bottle of the stuff.

I've made my peace with that little voice.

I don't mind taking care of Orlando. In fact, I'm grateful for the cheat sheet. He saved my life all those years ago. If I can make his life easier by pouring him a glass of painfully dry red wine, I am happy to do so.

When he comes out freshly showered and smelling like my vanilla body wash, his tensed shoulders loosen in a gust. "You made dinner."

I sit back down to resume working on my project. "I sure did. It's my night. Taco Tuesday. Nothing but the best for you, Orlando my love." It's a joke, clearly. All I did was made a few quesadillas, brown some meat and onions, chop up a tomato and lettuce, and put out some sour cream and salsa.

He sits down, looking truly touched that I cooked. "Thanks, Coco my dove." He takes a few bites, and with each one, I feel him relaxing.

I don't want to ask him for blood. He just got home. Plus, I haven't found a polite way to request such a thing. My fingers are stiff and my neck aches. My limbs aren't trembling, thank goodness, but there is a chill in the room I cannot shake.

"Rome told me about what happened with Nico," Orlando says between bites. "I personally would have jumped on the opportunity to kick his teeth in, but that's why I'm not you. Your way is better. Longer thinking."

I appreciate his assessment of my actions. "Thanks. Believe me, the temptation to slap some sense into Nico is always there, but it can't be about me. It can't be about my anger or what I am owed. It's about Mayfield. It's about the vampire people. They need to see our families getting along again. That's when there was peace in Mayfield. We set the tone." I keep my eyes on the labels I am sticking on the silver bottles. "But don't worry. I got my licks in. He's got a busted rib that I aggravated. I'm not entirely selfless."

Orlando snorts. "Yes, you are." He drinks his wine and closes his eyes, sighing contentedly. "I haven't had tempranillo in a while. No matter what I'm eating, it always goes well."

I keep my eyes on my task while I work, kneeling in the living room while Orlando eats on a stool at the counter in the kitchen. There's just enough distance so he can eat sloppily without an audience, but not so much space that either of us has to raise our voices to be heard.

I stick a label on the silver bottle. "I'm glad you like the wine. You've been working far too hard. When you're here, you're off the clock. You get wine, a firm mattress and fuzzy pajamas."

He glances at me over his shoulder, then angles his body so he can eat while watching me work. "You know I don't wear fuzzy pajamas."

"You do tonight. Check your room. I picked up a pair on my way home. The house is drafty and it's freezing out, even though it's not snowy. You need something warmer."

He stands up and fetches a second wine glass from the cupboard, pouring half a glass and setting it at the seat beside him.

I keep working, but my fingers slip. This is taking so much longer than it would if I could feel my fingertips. I have to get up in four hours, and I still have dozens of bottles left to label.

"Have a drink with me," Orlando offers, sitting back down to help himself to more food.

"I'm good. You get that whole bottle to yourself. I smelled it when I was opening it to aerate it. I worry my entire mouth might turn into the Sahara if I try it." I shake my head at his chuckle. "I didn't realize wine came that dry."

"You might like it now." He jerks his head in silent invitation. "It's got my blood in it." He holds up his wrist, which has a napkin pressed to it.

That's all the invitation I need. It could be sewage in the glass, but if it had Orlando's blood in it, I would happily drink the whole thing.

I migrate to the counter and sit beside him on a stool, taking a longer drink than I would normally enjoy of the red wine. My lashes flutter shut as warmth races through my body. A gooey heat fills my fingertips with the relief they crave.

"Good, right? Rome always complains that it's too dry, but I like it."

I take another drink, gulping it down until it's gone. "It's not the wine, which is maliciously dry, by the way. Your blood..." I slump in my seat, resting my forehead on the table while my body thanks me for giving it what it needs. All my tension is gone in a gust, leaving me boneless and sleepy. "I needed that."

Orlando swears. "Why didn't you say something? I didn't realize it was that bad."

"It's not. I was just cold and stiff, is all." I moan softly to myself. "But now I'm warm and noodly."

"Noodly?"

"Mm-hm."

Orlando chuckles as he stands. "I think it's time to turn in, little noodle."

"I have to finish." But my protest is weak. In fact, I don't put up any more of a fight than that when Orlando bends at the knees and wraps my arm around his shoulders. He hoists me up in his arms, cradling me like a damsel as he carries me to my bedroom.

This is the life. I mean, not the turf wars and blatant bigotry running rampant through our city. Not the feud between our families. Not the work that's piled so high, there never seems to be an end to it all. But this moment of being carried behind closed doors envelopes my heart in a warmth that I hope never leaves me.

I would never have guessed Orlando could be this playful and sweet, but when he rests me on my bed, I see my friend in a new light. He's careful as he tucks me in, even going so far as kissing my forehead. "Goodnight, Coco."

I think I mumble a parting greeting, but I can't be sure. I'm too tired, too content, too filled with wine and blood to care about anything anymore.

I drift off to sleep, grateful for our bond and all it brings to my life.

8

BROTHERLY LOVE

The four hours wasn't quite enough sleep, though that is no surprise. I wake in a panic, thinking of all I still have left to do when I went to bed prematurely. My shower is quick, my hair thrown in a ballerina bun. I race to the living room to slap the rest of the labels onto the bottles.

Only when I get there, the work is already done. My mouth falls open, flabbergasted that anyone could be so thoughtful. Orlando must have finished the job after I fell asleep.

Does the man ever stop working?

Gratitude swarms in my soul as I stack the empty bottles in the boxes and move them quietly into my car. I don't want to wake Orlando, so my steps are measured until I get into my car and pull out onto the dirt road.

I am grateful Orlando and Rome ruled that the rebellion from Nico's people in the West End, as well as the threat from the revolution, has settled enough that I can drive without an escort. That was starting to get annoying.

I thought I would feel resentful about the mate bond between myself and Orlando, but I am enjoying it far more than I thought I might. Instead of frantic energy, I take as much calm as I can muster into the kitchenette in the backroom of the salon. It's not hard to pop open the boxes, fill the bottles and slide a dozen shampoos inside. In fact, I use the time to filter out unnecessary angst and distracting thoughts.

This is *my* business, and I am actively working on expanding it. I can do this.

I can do this, plus help reform local government.

Am I thinking too small? If the governor is willing to intervene as she has done, perhaps there are more people with even more power who are ready to throw their weight behind a positive change.

No, no. Local government first, then I can expand our reach. No point in proving to the world that vampires are humane if we're still dealing with turf wars and bigotry on the home front.

When I get lost, I turn to my mother. Even though I never knew her, there is enough news footage of her for me to get a good picture of who she was and how she did things. I reach for my phone and find one of the many videos of a press conference she gave.

Meeting with the Prime Minister is a big deal for anyone, but my mother's face is composed in the picture that floats over the article.

As often happens when I am lost, I find a photo of her that I like, then I search that image to see how many times it appears, and who covered the story. It is no surprise that the basic news channels each did a spin on this story, with some recaps ranging from "Chondra Kennedy Talks the Prime Minister into Paying for Vampire Sensitivity Training for Staff" to the more ludicrous "The Last Dead-blood—Woman or Witch? See who's really running our country into the ground".

Then something snags my eyes that I usually skip over as unimportant. Aside from the reputable and more conspiratorial news channels, there are a slew of fashion magazines that come up as having used a version of that picture of my mother.

Normally I only delve into those when I want to admire my mother's poise and beauty, but today I see it from a different angle.

Yes, the fashion magazines are largely talking about who designed her dress, what jewelry she is wearing, and the perfect complement her shoes always are, but smattered in the lines are clips from my mother that actually made it into the report. "Justice for none until there is justice for all," rings out as a beacon of importance amid the silk and lace.

I jot down the name of the designers mentioned as a plan begins to formulate on the fly. Sure, people watch me because I am now the Last Deadblood, but my mother made it so that people watched her because she had something important to say. When they were in danger of losing interest, she dressed herself up so that no one could dare look away.

I wonder if the sheriff saved any of her more lavish or expensive dresses.

Pride runs down my spine. I am going to fast track this education reform plan and I will get half of Mayfield's public works budget allocated to the West End, so help me.

Everyone paid attention to my mother, and thereby listened to what she said. The world began to change for the better because she played hard and used every tool at her disposal. At least, that's the story I've gleaned from researching her life. She helped negotiate policies and did so in the highest couture.

I can do that. I *need* to do that. I need eyes on the inequality. If I can keep my game face on, then I can make it so that if all eyes are on me, the people will be hearing about the inequality.

I am completely alone with my thoughts, and content to be so, until I hear footsteps in the salon.

My stylists aren't due for another two hours. I came in

early specifically so I could get this done without hindering their work.

I don't want to be a girl who has guns hidden in convenient places, but when situations like this arise, I know exactly what to do.

I hate that my life is such a mess that I know how to arm myself when someone breaks in.

My shoes slide off, so I don't make noise as I walk through the back kitchenette into my office. The gun stowed under my desk unhitches soundlessly from its hiding place. I keep the weapon aimed down and away from my body as I walk toward the idiot who thinks I might be an easy mark.

My door doesn't open soundlessly, but I am prepared, standing to the side while it swings open.

"Coco?" comes my eldest brother's voice.

Frustration sweeps through me like a fire ready to consume all the sweet things I sometimes envision myself to be. "Are you insane?"

Fintan holds up his hands when he sees my gun pointed to the side as I emerge. "Are *you* insane? Put the gun down."

"What the heck, Fintan? At what point do you think it's a good idea to break into my building?"

"I knocked."

"You did not. I would have heard you. And I have a

phone you could have called. Breaking in isn't an option unless the building is on fire."

Fintan's expression is not as repentant as I think he should be when caught being a tool. "What door did you come in through this morning when you got here?"

I motion to the rear of the salon. "The back door, near where I parked."

"Then you didn't see the note on your front door?"

My breath quickens. "No."

Fintan takes a folded piece of paper from his pocket and shows it to me.

Though the safety is on, I don't put my gun away, preferring to carry it if people can break in willy-nilly. I scan the paper, which was printed from any old printer, and typed on any old computer.

MADAM DEADBLOOD,

YOU'VE CARRIED ON LONG ENOUGH. YOUR FRATERNIZING WITH the enemy will cost you dearly.

-THE REVOLUTION

9

THE SHERIFF'S REQUEST

*I*ce courses through my veins when I take in the threat on the paper, but I do my best to keep any reaction to myself. "Great. Just great. You're taking it to the sheriff, right?"

Fintan rolls his shoulders back, glancing around the empty salon. "I was going to take it to Lampert."

I harrumph. "Take it to the sheriff, not his suck up second in command. Jaren Lampert only cares about getting a promotion and arresting vampires. He's the worst."

Fintan casts me a look of sheer irritation. "I don't talk bad about your friends."

"To be fair, my friends are good people. Jaren is annoying. Take that threat to the sheriff, Fintan."

"Fine, fine." He motions around the salon. "You need to set the alarm when you're in here working alone."

"Clearly." I frown at my brother, wondering why the two of us have never been close. How did Declan turn out compassionate and normal, yet Fintan breaks into people's businesses and somehow expects a thanks? "Did you stop by to get your hair cut? Because we don't open for another few hours."

He snorts, as if my profession is a joke. "No. I came by because I haven't had a chance to touch base with you since you got back."

"I must have missed your many phone calls." It's clear sarcasm. Fintan never calls me.

"Thought stopping by would be best. See how you are in person. You can lie to me over the phone."

"I can lie to you just as easily in person. Watch." I brighten my countenance. "Fintan, it's so good to see you!"

Fintan rolls his eyes. "Hilarious. Dad and I want an explanation about what you're doing, taking up with a Valentino."

I quirk an eyebrow up at my brother, gun still clutched to the side. He needs a haircut. My goodness, his bangs are hanging in his face.

I cock my hip to the side. "Declan told me he filled you both in. Did you need some explanation other than me doing what I've always tried to do? Repairing relations between the vampires and the humans sometimes requires drastic action."

"Apparently. This is a bad idea, Coco. You're not just

playing with fire anymore, opening up a shop where you know you shouldn't. You're walking straight through the inferno, expecting not to get burned."

I lift my chin in defiance of my small-minded brother who will never see beauty in the world the way I do. "You're wrong on that, Fintan. I don't expect I won't get burned. I know I will. I just don't care. This whole thing is about more than just me and my safety. It's about an entire people who don't get their needs met or even heard."

His rounder nose twitches. "This is dangerous."

"This is necessary."

"Find a better way!"

I don a bland smile and blink up at his rising temper. "Well, I tried asking nicely, but some people don't like to hear that they need to grow up. Funny, right?"

Fintan holds my gaze in that way he does when he is keeping himself back from being a true jackass. "I don't care how you end it but end it publicly and end it now. A human dating a vampire, even to make a point, is disgusting."

His words are more pointed than usual and filled with vitriol. Though I've known Fintan feels this way about vampires, in my childlike imagination, I hoped he would have been at least working toward ambivalence, instead of this chip on his shoulder that's sure to give him a permanent scowl.

"I thought you were better than that."

Fintan shakes his head, as if he wants to say the exact same thing to me. "Stop this, Coco. Your behavior already got you put into hiding."

I know I should stop myself, but my words bubble up until I set them free. "Mom wouldn't have backed down."

Fintan's nostrils flare at the taboo topic. "And how would you know? You never even met the woman. The doctors warned her two kids was enough. Her body wouldn't be able to handle having a third. But she *had* to have a girl. Had to push herself beyond reason, just like you always manage to do. When she was pregnant with you, she was never the same. The shakes got worse. Everything got worse. Learn from Mom's mistake, Coco. Pushing yourself this hard is going to be your undoing." It's a well-aimed dagger to my heart, but his next words ensure that I will be bleeding for years to come. "If having you didn't kill her, the vampires surely would have. She was a danger to them, and so are you. It's only a matter of time before they get tired of the sword hanging over their heads. As long as you walk the earth, they will want you dead, no matter how badly you want to save the three-legged mongrels of the world."

His words hollow me out, taking all the confidence from me with a gut punch I should have seen coming. Fintan doesn't like when people call him out. His bite carries too much cruelty for me to withstand.

"Get out," I whisper, my words clearly enunciated.

Fintan's eyes widen, as if he's only just realized what he said. "Coco, I didn't mean..."

"Get out!" This time I scream at him, unwilling to tolerate another second of him saying the same things that I use to belittle myself.

If my mother hadn't had me, she wouldn't have died so young.

I am the reason my mother didn't see her sons live past elementary age.

Fintan holds up his hands and exits without further drama, leaving me alone with my self-loathing.

I had all the focus in the world this morning when I started, but now as I return to the shampoos and conditioners, my movements are labored.

One project at a time, I remind myself. Hating myself for getting my mother killed will have to wait. Packaging up the shampoos and conditioners were next on the list, so that's what I do my best to accomplish.

My mind is racing through grief as I work on the task at hand, slogging through the job with precious little personal power. Though this whole thing hurts my heart, I manage to get everything boxed and shoved into my car.

When my father calls as I drive to my third destination of the morning, it takes me until the fourth ring to pick up. "Hey, Sheriff. If you're calling to tell me to apologize to Fintan, you can tell him he can find his apology in the garbage, where I also threw my self-respect when he talked to me the way he did."

It's not the best greeting, but I'm in no mood for subtleties.

My father lets out a long sigh. "Oh, jeez. What did your brother do this time?"

"He's just being his charming self. Hates me for being me, wants me to be less me. You know, the usual."

"I'm actually calling because your brother turned in the note he found at your salon this morning. I'll be stopping by in an hour to take a look at the place. I didn't want to spook you, showing up unannounced in uniform."

"That's fine. I figured you might need to do that."

There's a pause before my father speaks again. "Are you alright?"

"I'm always fine."

"I'm sure you are. You disappeared on me. Declan filled us in, but I couldn't get ahold of you for weeks."

I'm not sure why that's worth noting. He went weeks without contacting me when I lived overseas. Whole years, actually. "Yup."

I'm not about to fill in the gaps of silence, since he is the one who called.

"Before you left, I mentioned starting up a regular family dinner at my place. Does that still work for you?"

I try to reach back that far in my memory. Though it

was only a few weeks ago, it feels like months. "Family night?"

"That's right. I'll cook. You just show up and do your best not to tear Fintan a new one."

I let out a chuckle that sneaks up on me. My father never makes me laugh. Huh. "No promises. But sure, family dinner night. Sounds... fun." I don't know how to quantify in words how horrible it sounds, so I go for a fib.

It sounds awful, awkward and unnecessary. Declan and I talk every day and see each other a few times a week. Fintan and I see each other rarely, which is far too often. I see my father more than I've seen him in the years I was away. Though, thanks to the biweekly meetings between my father and Rome being moved to a different location, I won't see my father as often.

I rub the nape of my neck as I switch lanes and speed up. I have a meeting tomorrow that I should be preparing for, but I've been away from my business for too long. I am determined to put in a full day and then get my notes together this evening.

One way or another, this world will change for the better.

I only hope I can keep up.

10

THE FINAL VOTE

I did not sleep well last night. Going over my notes took far longer than I was hoping, coupled with making time for my new obsession: to channel my mother and become a force for change. It took seventeen phone calls to get in touch with one of the designer's secretaries, and eighteen to connect with the coveted designer herself.

Orlando listened quietly while I pitched the designer my reason for calling: that my mother's dream to see the humans behave humanely toward the vampires is not dead, but very much alive in me. With her help, I would like to draw more eyes toward me while I campaign for the cause of equality.

Ming Lu designed clothes for my mother, and still has an active and well-respected couture brand. Together, we can garner public favor. While they are gaping at my clothing, they will be listening to my plea for change.

It's time to pull out all the stops, since the governor still hasn't made good on pushing through the education reform proposal even after the picture of me snuggling up to a Valentino went viral.

I remember ending the call last night with a winded grin, and Orlando commenting, "I don't think I've ever heard you talk so fast. Well done."

Even as we drive to City Hall where the negotiations are to take place on the education proposal, I still feel the thrill of taking one more step toward becoming my mother's daughter. "I can't believe Ming Lu is going to send over a tailor today to take my measurements. It's all so surreal."

Orlando's head bobs as if he cares about things like designer outfits. "How could she say no? You were very convincing. I think it was just a matter of you needing to be ready. There are more people who believe in the cause than just us. Most of those people don't live in Mayfield, granted, but they're out there." Orlando pulls into the parking lot, his face suddenly more serious than usual as he cuts the engine. "I have a confession to make."

My stomach drops. "Oh, jeez. What?"

He motions to the parked black sedan with tinted windows that matches his own. "You kept saying this week that when the *two* of us go in and sit down with the heads of Mayfield, when the *two* of us talk to them... You had to know Rome would be here, right?"

My mouth falls open. "Does this look like the face of a girl in the know? Why is he here?"

"Because this is just as much his fight as it is yours. And you know you need him here. People respect him too much to counter him with any real authority."

My upper lip curls. "And I don't demand respect?"

Orlando leans his head back, closing his eyes. "Look, I know you hate this, but like you've been saying: this is bigger than you. Bigger than Rome. It deserves our best people on the job. You are the best that humanity has to offer." He motions to the twin vehicle as Rome steps out of it and buttons his suit jacket, looking like he's crushed a million hearts without ever managing to grow one for himself. "And Rome is the best my kind has to offer."

I take in a deep breath, for a second debating whether or not I should cut and run. "You're a jerk for springing this on me."

"I've been called worse. And I didn't want to chance you chickening out and bailing on the whole thing." He taps the steering wheel. "Let's snap this off today, Coco. It's been weeks they've been hemming and hawing about putting through this change. Time to bring in the big guns and put this thing to rest."

Several arguments bubble up in my chest, but none dare come out. They would all sound selfish if they did.

I drag in a deep breath, then let it out like a hissing tire through pursed lips. "It's not about me. You're right. This is necessary. We'll do the job and be done."

Orlando wets his lower lip with the tip of his tongue. "Have you told him about…" He motions between the two of us.

I squirm in my seat. "Not yet. I can do that after the meeting. Sorry for putting it off."

Orlando moves his hand from left to right across his body. "No need to apologize. I was going to suggest we do it together. It was cowardly of me to send you in to do the dirty work. I don't want to tell him any more than you do. Maybe it won't be so bad if the two of us do it together."

I let out a breath I didn't realize I was holding in. "Thanks."

When my door opens, I startle. Then I roll my shoulders back, greeting Rome with a succinct nod as I get out of the car. He offers his hand, but I don't take it.

I don't need it.

There is a reporter who apparently knew we would be here today. I indulge him in a few photos with me walking between Orlando and Rome as we move toward the city building.

"You look lovely, Colette," Rome offers when we enter.

"Shut up," I snap. I dressed in a cream fitted button-down, a navy pinstripe pencil skirt and matching stilettos to look my best for this meeting, not to impress him. My hair is pulled back in a knot that Rachel promised made me look like a shark ready to take down my prey.

Though Rome would never dare look disheveled in public, there is a marked exhaustion to him, coloring the bags under his eyes. He shaved this morning, finally scraping off the growth that made him look compromised. He smells like the aftershave that haunts my dreams.

I try to push every memory of our time together from my brain so I can keep myself upright.

The children. I need to make sure the vampire children are granted equal educational opportunities. That is my goal.

I am not leaving City Hall without a deal this time.

My briefcase remains at my side until we reach the conference room where the mayor is already waiting for us, along with the two heads of the school boards in Mayfield, the secretary treasurer of the city and a handful of reporters.

Mayor Stapleton stands to greet us, making a point to shake only my hand, though he shows respect by dipping his head toward Rome and meeting Orlando's stalwart gaze.

Orlando pulls out my chair for me and then positions himself to stand at the exit, where he is most comfortable.

Rome sits beside me, leaning into his placement of power at the foot of the table. His elbow graces the armrest as he surveils the others, making it clear that nothing will go down without his approval.

The mayor resumes his seat. "The governor just arrived. She'll be in shortly."

Rome acts as if the news means nothing to him. As much as I loathe having him beside me, he is good at these sorts of power plays. Having a good, altruistic idea means nothing if you cannot get it implemented.

His gaze zeroes in on the secretary treasurer, who has been one of the resistant cogs in the machine. If we can get him more compliant, then it won't matter that Marjorie—the head of the East End's Board of Education—doesn't want to split the education budget evenly.

Rome knows this full well. He does his silent job of intimidating the secretary treasurer into losing his bearings with a mixture of cool looks and pointed glares.

I try not to smirk when the secretary treasurer drops his pen on the floor.

We have had enough meetings. I resolve myself to not leave this gathering until something is signed and change is initiated. I don't have time to be jerked around.

I really don't have the patience for sitting beside my former boyfriend beyond today.

When Governor Ingrid Mason shows up, the two of us join the others in standing to show our respect. We don't sit until she does. Then the meeting begins.

I don't expect shouting. I don't expect total agreement,

either. But as the hours tick by, I grow weary of the tedious back and forth, worrying this will just be another meeting. The governor was supposed to hold up her end of the bargain, but I won't know how long her reach is until the final vote happens.

I have compromised on nothing, which shouldn't be a surprise to anyone in the room.

"Look here," says Marjorie as she flips her dyed blonde hair over her shoulder, "we've given you enough. We simply can't educate children on half the budget we are currently using. We can come down a little, but it's a poor investment to divert our funds to the West End. The dropout rate is astronomical for young vampires. They are simply not worth the investment!"

"Are you insane?" The Board of Education Director for the West End seems to have found his bravery, now that we have shown we are going to see this thing through till the end. Perhaps that's all Christopher needed—just a little backup. "We underinvest in the West End's education, and we're surprised when they don't put more value in school than the adults do? If you're expecting the children to lead the way, perhaps you should learn to listen to them first. They drop out because the poverty level is higher. They drop out to get jobs. There are many problems holding the West End back from prospering, but attitudes like yours are the biggest contributors to the rot of social conscience."

The plan devolved into arguing a while ago, but the

governor and Rome have largely stayed out of it. Not until Rome raises his hand to call for silence does the bickering come to an end.

I want to be able to do that.

Rome doesn't raise his voice; he doesn't have to. "Here's how this is going to go. We're going to vote now on this thing. I'm not wasting another minute here unless it involves talking action steps. You vote this down, we're taking it higher." He points to the others in the room. "We don't need you to get this done. You can either be part of the change or be forced into it, and consequently out of office. I personally don't care which you choose, but we're choosing now."

The mayor harrumphs. "You can't just call a vote like that; it's my job."

"Then do your job." Rome folds his fingers over his abdomen, sitting back in his seat. "Vote now. Madam Deadblood and I will not compromise that the budget should be split evenly. Stop wasting your breath pretending you have credible arguments."

I can tell the mayor does not like that Rome has taken control of the room, but everyone casts their votes the old fashion way, by raising their hands when the mayor calls for the powers that be to choose sides.

I hold my breath because, as much as we have been invited into this room, we do not get a vote. Only the officials get to decide if the city of Mayfield will put its money where its mouth is, and care about the children who live within their city limits.

Anger shoots through me unexpectedly. The fact that this is our millionth pitch and there is still resistance means we, as humans, have failed. The fact this is even an issue that requires massive change means the humans have neglected to be humane. No matter how the vote turns out, we have already lost.

Bile rises in my throat when I realize how small this step is, and how many more need to be orchestrated. My fingers curl around my armrests, squeezing as fury blazes in what is left of my soul.

I will not live long enough to see all the changes I am fighting for come to fruition. But I am firm in my resolve that I will not leave the world worse than I found it. If I cannot have children of my own, then I will protect the ones in my hometown.

Let that be my legacy.

I close my eyes and wait to see how the chips fall, knowing that no matter what, the work toward social justice will never be done.

11

TELLING ROME THE TRUTH

Orlando surprises me when he breaks from his stoic demeanor the moment we make it to the parking lot. "I can't believe you did it."

"*We* did it," I correct him, breathless from the slim but firm win. "I'm still reeling."

Rome's smile is only for us, and only because no one is in the parking lot to see it. They're all still inside, doling out responsibilities. "And it's starting so soon. I really thought they were going to kick it out a few months."

Though there is joy in Orlando's expression, I know the gavel of reality is about to fall. "The three of us have a lot to celebrate. Get on in, Rome. We're going out, and I'm driving."

It's a ruse. I mean, obviously. Going out for drinks or food and telling Rome the truth about our mated friendship would be a terrible move. Any public place would be a disaster.

But the three of us get into Orlando's car, with Rome alone in the backseat. The victory of our win is short-lived. My palms begin to sweat as my fight or flight instinct kicks in.

Orlando must sense this, because he pulls out onto the main road and sets the child locks so I can't jump out of the moving vehicle.

I shoot him a look of pure panic. "Maybe we shouldn't…"

But Orlando is not deterred. Asking him to keep the secret from his cousin for this long is more than I should have expected of my big sweetie pie. This isn't just happening to me; this is his life forever changed, as well.

Rome's smile fades as he takes in the shifting tenor of the car. "Are we celebrating? Because neither of you look terribly vivacious right now. You look like you're driving us to our doom, Orlando."

Orlando's reply is grave as he keeps his eyes on the road. "We're not going to celebrate. In fact, I'm not sure you'll want to do much celebrating ever again after this."

Rome leans his head back, letting out an exasperated groan. "Are you kidding me? Can't we have this one day? Do you know how few wins we get? I thought…" He runs his hands over his face, sighing heavily. "Alright, lay it on me."

I paw at the door, fruitlessly trying to open it so I can jump out of the vehicle. "Orlando, I don't like this! He's going to flip out!"

Orlando does the dirty work because that is what the situation requires. "Rome, do you remember the day you took off?"

Rome turns his chin to the side, staring out the window. "That's what we're bringing up right now? Are you kidding me? She hates me enough as it is." Then Rome leans forward, his hand cupping my bicep.

It's an intrusion, for sure, but I don't have the wherewithal to shake him off.

"Coletta, I was wrong. I was scared something impossible was happening, so I ran. I was foolish and childish and every other stupid thing a man can possibly be when he forgets he is not a boy anymore. Leaving you when you could barely breathe and had no idea what might have happened was the worst thing I could have done. If I never stop paying for it, I will understand."

It's a grand apology, and more than I expected I would let him get out before dismissing his words completely. "I don't want to talk about it."

I glare at Orlando, though I'm not mad at him. Not really. I'm scared that the meager amount of stability we have established is about to go up in flames.

Orlando is the only grownup in the car, apparently, because he delivers the hard truth without holding back.

"You left Coco. She couldn't breathe, and you left. It doesn't matter how scared you were. She needed you there."

Rome squeezes my bicep. "I know! I can't tell you how many nights I spent hating myself for doing that to you. It's not even possible, what I thought was happening. You were probably choking on your gum or something, and I left you to struggle through that. You could have died because I was a coward. Coletta, you deserve better, so I came back, aiming to be better."

Orlando grips the steering wheel. No matter how much I beg him with my eyes to stop talking, he cracks Rome's world with a few simple sentences. "You thought the mating ritual was taking place, didn't you."

Rome nods. "It was stupid. It's not even possible. I spooked myself and left you completely vulnerable. Coletta, vampire mating is just about the worst thing for a man in my position. It's..."

"I know what vampire mating is," I tell him, my throat dry.

Orlando fills in the gaps so there is no confusion. "That's exactly what was happening, Rome. The two of you were mid-mating. When you left, I went in there and saw she was barely breathing. Her body was in crisis without her mate's blood to seal the ritual."

Rome freezes, his hand motionless on my arm.

I wonder how much he is absorbing.

After a few beats of stunned silence, Rome shakes his

head. "That's not possible. She's a human! Orlando, you're wrong. Humans can't mate with a vampire. It's called the vampire mating bond for a reason!" His eyes glisten with unshed tears.

Orlando keeps his voice measured. "I'm just as in the dark as you are on the subject. I thought it was impossible, too, but apparently, we were both wrong. Coco was trying to mate with you, or you were trying to mate with her. Either way, it happened."

"You're my mate?" Rome asks me, true fear crashing with wonder in his voice.

A squeak of surprise is all I can get out when Rome lunges forward between the two front seats and jerks my chin to the side. He kisses me so hard and so deep; I nearly vomit from the intense swell of emotions.

My body stills, braces, falls into the kiss, and then tears away from him with a scream that reveals a heart sufficiently dismembered. "No!"

Orlando swerves but manages to keep us from crashing. "Sit down, you idiot," he shouts to his cousin. "Do you think we would be this upset if the story ended there?"

Rome is the perfect picture of shock. "It's happened. I thought it would be the worst thing in the world, but I was wrong. Being without you was the worst thing in the world, tré-sur. These past few weeks have been agony."

I cling to the door, my lower lip trembling. He's saying all the right things, but about a month too late.

Being tied to me isn't a horror the man I love should fear.

It seems Rome is rapidly coming to that revelation, now that he is being faced with his worst fear and seeing it was merely a shadow of a problem. It was not a terror that should have ruled his choice to run away from me.

Still, it's too little too late.

Rome sits back but keeps his hand on my bicep, rubbing this time to soothe my angst. "Coletta, I will take care of everything. Whatever you need, it's yours. Whatever you want, it's yours. When you forgive my stupidity, we can finish the mating ritual and I will be yours forever. I already am, but the vampire bond gives…"

"I know all about the vampire bond," I choke out, tears clouding my vision. "I swear, if you say one more romantic thing to me, I will throw you out this very window. You left me."

"Punish me as harsh as you like. We will get through this."

Orlando was bold before but now he's gone mute.

I don't want to deliver this final blow, but it's too permanent a thing not to tell him now. "You were gone. Like, gone, gone. I didn't realize what had happened, but my body…" I swallow hard. "I was ice cold. After a day or two, I could barely calm down. I couldn't sleep. Orlando noticed and… I didn't realize his blood was in my tea."

Orlando picks up where I fall short on courage. "I fed

her my blood. It was either that or lose her forever. I waited for you as long as I could. I told you to come home." He rubs the nape of his neck. "She was deteriorating, Rome. It wasn't my intention to bond with her, but it was either that or watch her wither and die. I figured I could seal the two of you together because I knew eventually you would come around. My blood can't be all that dissimilar from yours." He clears his throat. "Apparently the bond can tell the difference, because the ritual is complete, and it chose me as her mate."

Rome's hand falls away from my arm as a tidal wave of shock knocks him back. "You... And you... And then you... So now you're..."

I didn't want Rome anywhere near me before, but suddenly I feel cold where his hand should be.

"Mated," Orlando confirms. "Obviously there's nothing more to it than that. I live with her still, which was the arrangement before it all happened. We're friends. I had no intention of moving in on your girlfriend. That's not going to change."

"I know that," Rome whispers, leaning back in his seat. "Give me a minute."

Now the tears really start to fall. All my anger at Rome is probably still there to some degree, but right now all I want is to fall into his arms and hear him lie to me. I want Rome to tell me that everything is going to be okay, even though we both know it's not.

"Who else knows? Nico doesn't, that's for sure."

"Only Declan and a friend of his," Orlando answers, keeping true to his word not to out Declan to anybody. "It's not exactly something we want spread around. We're both still trying to wrap our minds around it all. The vampire mating bond is more legend than reality. Bringing something like that to light with such an unexpected twist to it isn't a roller coaster the world is ready to ride."

Rome motions between us. "The picture of the two of you, looking all cozy together."

"Was staged, just like I told you before," Orlando confirms. "It was supposed to be you. Declan tried to make it unclear if it was you or me with her. The governor wouldn't agree to push the education proposal through unless Coco was seen dating a Valentino. We thought Nico would be the next best thing, what with you being gone, but that didn't go over so well with Nico, as you know. I was the only Valentino left, so I did my duty."

Orlando's words are true and fine, but they smack me across the face because I am too vulnerable to tell the difference between hurt and reality.

I cover my mouth to stifle a sob.

Orlando is my big sweetie pie, while I am his duty.

Orlando softens. "I didn't mean it like that. I misspoke. Pretending to be your arm candy isn't a duty. It's…"

"I know," I reply, waving off his apology. "I'm just upset about it all right now."

"Deep breaths," Orlando reminds me. "This was never going to go over well. Give him time. We've had weeks to process, and we still get tripped up from time to time."

I nod, but no part of me wants to be in the car any longer. "Can you take me home? I just want to go to sleep. I can't be in this conversation anymore."

Orlando purses his lips but turns on the next street. "Of course. The hard part is over. We told him."

But it seems that Rome has left his body. No one speaks the rest of the way to my house. When I get out, Orlando stays in the car, no doubt to drive Rome back to his.

I drop my keys twice in my effort to unlock the door. My tears are a hazard now, impairing my vision so much that when the door pops open, I stumble through the house without bothering to take off my coat or shoes. My briefcase hits the floor of my bedroom as I collapse onto my bed so I can bury my tears in the silk of my pillow.

Yes, that could have gone better.

12

MING LU'S BLESSING

At no point do I want Rome in my home, but when I hear his voice coming from the kitchen, I don't get up to shoo him away. We've all been through an extreme high and a dismal low today. I don't have it in me to begrudge anyone a little respite in my home if it grants them peace. At least Orlando and Rome are talking about it all without me having to be part of it.

I'm still atop my covers with my coat and shoes on, wondering how it happened that my life got so off-course. If I was living overseas and hadn't got it in my mind that Mayfield needed my interference, none of this would be happening. I hate when I agree with my father and Fintan, but right now, I worry I have made the wrong choice by moving here.

Declan and I text for a bit so I can bring him up to

speed. He's driving an hour away to go on a date with Lucas tonight, which he tells me he is looking forward to.

I wish my brother didn't have to drive an hour out of town to date his boyfriend. I wonder how the sheriff would react if he knew that Declan was gay. Maybe it wouldn't be as bad as Declan is thinking. Or, worst case scenario, Declan doesn't have the sheriff in his life anymore.

I gotta say, I lived like that for years, and it wasn't so bad.

But different situations and all that. I wonder how long my brother will be able to keep up his secret before the whole thing exhausts him.

I'm on the edge of giving up on everything myself until the doorbell rings. I don't bother getting up because Orlando answers the door for me. It's not until his fist raps on my door that I consider rejoining the world.

"I'm coming in, Coco." When he walks into my bedroom, he frowns. "You still have your coat and shoes on. You laid down like that?"

"Too much work," I whine, playing up the theatrics so we don't have to talk about how rough that conversation in the car was. "Who's at the door?"

"Someone from Ming Lu? Said he's supposed to take your measurements. Is that a thing?"

I stand, shedding my coat because I have to rejoin the world at some point. Might as well be now. "Yeah. Thank you." I know I look like I've been crying, but I am not about to let that stop the plan I set into motion. I had high hopes for this arrangement, back when I had far more optimism.

When I move out of my bedroom toward the living room, I do my best not to let Rome's presence ruffle me. I extend my hand to the fifty-something man with gray whisps around his temples and black, coiffed hair on top. "Good afternoon, sir. Thank you for coming."

"Absolutely. I am Jung-hoon. I'm going to take your measurements, then I'll be on my way. But since it's for Ming Lu, I'll feel better if I do everything twice. We want to get this exactly right."

"Absolutely. She's the best."

He has joy shining in his eyes—a stark contrast to my dismal weariness. "Forgive me, but Ming Lu played the recording of your conversation with her for me. For everyone who is working on this project, actually."

"This project?" My head tilts to the side. Good to know Ming Lu records her conversations. I should probably start doing that, in case the person leaving letters escalates to phone calls and whatnot. Now that I'm not talking salaciously to Rome anymore, I have no reason not to record my phone calls.

Jung-hoon takes out his tape. "Yes. Ming Lu flew me out specifically to take your measurements and oversee the fittings. There are two seamstresses who will sew everything you wear by hand. Ming Lu has already started on a few designs for your normal workwear."

My eyes widen, and suddenly Rome and Orlando shuffle to the back of my awareness. "I was hoping to wear some of her designs, but I didn't mean she had to start from scratch. Something she has already in her catalog would be more than sufficient."

Jung-hoon studies my flabbergast with kindness. "What you are doing—reminding humans to be humane—it's a lesson that goes beyond how we treat the vampires, though that is no small thing. It's an investment in our future you are making. Ming Lu respects your mission, as it is her own. She helped your mother get eyes on the cause of equality. Now that you are ready to take up your mother's mantle, Ming Lu will do all she can to help you, just as she helped your mother."

I am already too emotional from the car ride. To have this man exude such support and kindness, to have Ming Lu herself go so many extra miles to support this effort...

Perhaps it wasn't a mistake, me moving back to Mayfield. Maybe there are more than just two families fighting for a brighter future.

Perhaps peace is possible after all.

13

SORRY AND AFRAID

After Jung-hoon leaves, I resolve to put pen to paper and plan myself out of this funk. I am tempted to let defeat, agony and heartache overtake me, but I know that choice is long gone. I hide out in my bedroom with my laptop and a notepad, determined not to take the win we had today and call the world fixed.

This is step one of many.

Do I know much about social infrastructure? No. But that doesn't mean I can't learn. I start by gathering data, jotting down statistics gleaned from studying cities where crime is low, beautification is prioritized, and people report general satisfaction. While I know Mayfield is a different animal altogether, being that we have the entire vampiric population in our borders, that doesn't mean none of the pillars of success apply to us.

When I exhaust that topic, I switch to focusing on

cities that were in ruin years ago, but somehow managed to get themselves out of the dysfunctional rut. How did they do it?

What started out as a means to divert creeping depression is now blowing up into pages and pages of notes combined with strategy.

One facet of Mayfield is on its path to being fixed. Now it is time to tackle the next one, whatever that may be.

I lose track of the time, working uninterrupted until I hear a knock on my bedroom door. "Yeah?"

Rome stays in the doorway when he opens it. He is on the verge of entering but knows he is not welcome. "I'm ordering dinner for the three of us. Are you hungry for anything in particular?"

I keep my eyes on the screen of my laptop. "I'm hungry for everything in general. Whatever you choose is fine, but plan on me eating like a trucker."

Rome laughs airily through his nose. "Only you could find a way to make me smile."

The room is quiet as I keep my eyes on my work. I feel him watching me, but I don't draw attention to it. I don't mind him here, but I am not ready to talk about all the things that could have and should have gone better.

I am not sure I'm ready to look at him. I don't hate him, but it's painful to measure the divide between where we were a month ago against where we are now.

"Are you physically okay?" Rome asks me. "I don't

know how overbearing I'm allowed to be. It's too late for me to ask, but if you're willing to put up with my anxiety, I have questions."

I keep my back to him, though not with any hostile intent. I know that if I look at the most beautiful man in the world, I will forget that he is also selfish sometimes. I will forget that he left me high and dry because he was afraid.

I was afraid.

"You can ask questions, provided you can control yourself when you hear the answer."

Rome swallow hard. "I can do that."

I seriously doubt his claim, but I answer his question all the same. "Yes, I'm physically okay. Better than ever, actually. Orlando's blood pairs well with my medication. Makes my tremors disappear completely. But the relief seems to only last so long as I have his blood every night. If I skip nights, I go back to the problems I had before, only slightly worse."

He pauses a beat to digest the information. "Worse how?"

I purse my lips, reliving those days in the cabin where Orlando was too far away. "There's a cold I can't shake. I get my tremors back, but there's also a stiffness to me. Like the beginnings of hypothermia." I roll my shoulders, trying to shake off the memory. "I don't like it."

Another long pause. I'm glad Rome isn't rushing

through his queries. He seems to be actually listening without letting his ego, worry or opinions get in the way. "Orlando mentioned he pricks his wrist to put his blood in your tea. Is it enough? It's only a few drops. Would more help?"

I shrug. "It's all conjecture at this point. This isn't even supposed to be possible, so it's trial and error. But asking Orlando to give me more blood isn't exactly fair to him. I don't need more than he gives me."

Rome stays in the doorway, respecting my space while he invades my mind. He grips the doorjamb. "I have no right to ask this, but I'm selfish and out of sorts tonight, so I need to know. Do you love him?"

It's the first time I turn my head to look at Rome's lost expression. "Are you serious?"

He closes his eyes, his lashes thick and beguiling. "Serious and sorry, and so very lost."

And he looks every bit those three things. The bags under his eyes pair well with his slumped shoulders.

I narrow my eyes at him to scold his ridiculous question, though I have no trouble answering it. "I've always loved all three of you. You know that. But no, I don't have romantic feelings for Orlando, if that's what you're asking. Orlando is a decade older than me."

Rome throws his head back. "*I* am a decade older than you."

"That was different. I'm in love with you, so that didn't

matter. I'm not in love with Orlando. I should think that would be obvious. He's my friend." I don't want to diminish how important Orlando has become to me. "The bond makes us understand each other better, though. I can see how that could be misconstrued as falling in love. But it's not. Orlando is dear to me. I expect I will always feel that way. Even without the bond, Orlando matters a great deal to me. Always has."

Rome stills. "You love me?"

"That's all you got out of what I just said?" I shake my head. "Of course I'm in love with you. But that changes nothing. We are over." I don't say it with venom, but with a finality that rings through the bedroom.

His fingers curl around the wood of the doorjamb. "We ended, yes. But in time, perhaps we can begin again. Please, tré-sur. Give us time."

I don't rush the process of thinking through a response. "It's not worth it. Not for me and certainly not for you."

Rome's face sours. "It's worth it for me. I will do all I can to make us worth it for you."

I stand, unwilling to prolong the obvious. "My mother didn't live past thirty. Her mother didn't, either. It's a long line of women dying young. You know that Deadbloods have a low life expectancy. It's selfish of me to carry on with a man as serious as you." I roll my shoulders back. "I need some air. I'm going on a walk." I pick up my coat and slide my arms through it, pausing when Rome crosses the divide between us to zip it for me.

He smells of cinnamon but wreaks of sadness. It's hard to be near him and not fall into his arms, forgetting all that is broken between us. He is beautiful, his mere presence drawing me in and awakening parts of me I have fought hard to strangle and silence.

He stands close to me, straightening my sleeves because I haven't raised my hands to push him away.

"The Deadblood legacy is going to die with me," I whisper. "We can't have children together. Even if it were somehow possible, I will not allow it."

Rome thumbs my face, bringing tenderness so acute that it pains my soul to have him this close. "I decided a long time ago that I would not have children. Being with you isn't the reason, Coletta. I would not wish the responsibilities that have fallen to me on my son. I am not cheated, being with you." It's not until his thumb sweeps across the apple of my cheek that I realize there are tears dotting my face. "But I am cheated every day that I am not with you. No matter how much time we have left, I want to spend my life with you."

My lashes flutter shut. Rome is a poet with his words, but there is still too much pain to forge ahead. "You left me."

Rome's forehead presses to mine, his sweet breath fanning across my nose. "I was wrong."

My eyes squinch, my lips pursing against the pain of my words seconds before they come. "You are the reason I am bonded with Orlando."

It's perhaps meanspirited to pin that twist of fate on Rome, but if he had stayed, it stands to reason that the two of us would have been bonded instead.

Which I remember him calling "a fate worse than death."

"I wish it had been me," he whispers. "I thought being mated would be the worst thing that could happen to a man, but it turns out that being parted from you is the thing I should have feared. Please, Coletta. Don't turn me away."

I ball my toes in my shoes. "I don't forgive you."

"Of course we are the same, even in that. I don't forgive me, either."

I don't know why that strikes me as slightly comical, but I snort through a laugh that catches us both by surprise. "Good. Then we agree that you're in the doghouse."

"I'll be in whichever house you put me." Rome chips away at the ice surrounding my heart when he nuzzles his nose across mine. His lips move across mine, but neither of us seals the connection with a kiss. "Do not forgive me yet. Let me grovel a while. I have big groveling plans."

I can't help my smile, even if it comes with tears. "You do?"

His arm slides around my waist as he takes my hand and holds it out to the side. His hips marry themselves to mine as he turns us in a slow dance. There is no music, only magic, and just enough to carry us through.

His cheek presses to mine. "You are precious to me, Coletta."

For just this sliver of time, I let down my guard and allow myself to believe that second chances are real, and that true love can span the sea of wrongs stacked tall between us.

THE MAN I SHOULDN'T LOVE

$\mathcal{K}$eeping up with running a franchise is one headache I quite enjoy. Putting a line of my shampoos and conditioners for sale in a retail store is another fun challenge.

Juggling those two things with politics is becoming problematic, especially when my ex-boyfriend has it in his head that the best place to be is helping me.

"I can do this on my own," I tell Rome through gritted teeth. "It's not outside my wheelhouse to know how to clear out a pipe. The drains in my first salon in Lonmure clogged all the time, so I got pretty good at it."

"I can see that."

I feel vastly underdressed because Rome is always so sharply put together. I changed into my housework tank top and cutoffs, even though there is an inch of snow on the ground outside. There is an oil stain across the left breast and a plethora of paint splatter across the front of my top. When the garbage disposal refused to do its one job, I got out my grungy clothes and tools and went to work on the thing.

"I really don't mind helping," Rome offers again. It's as if it is physically painful for him to hold himself back from taking over and making the project his own.

"I'm sure you have better things to do than hang out in my kitchen. Go away; I've got this."

"I know you can fix the sink, but do you need to? I'm right here."

I slide out from under the sink to frown at him while I grab a wrench one size up. "Yes, you're right there. Funny coincidence, you being here. Orlando was supposed to make dinner tonight, but he just so happened to need to spend extra time in the West End."

Rome shoves his hands in his pockets, trying (and failing) to look innocent. "Orlando sent me to watch the house tonight in his place. He left you some cranberry juice with his blood in it, so you're not missing out on him being here."

"Uh-huh." I know exactly what Orlando is doing. He's putting Rome and me together in hopes that the ice that has crusted around my heart will soon thaw.

As if it's all so simple.

Everything from under the sink is on the counter, leaving the cavern bare for me to curl in and out of. It's actually bigger back here than I realized. I could probably store old rags under here, too.

I inch back under the sink on my back, positioning my flashlight as best I can. After the third time it tilts to an unhelpful spot, I growl at the thing. I scoop it up and shove it between my knees, which are crooked up, my legs bent up to try and aim the flashlight just so.

Rome's overly polite visage crumbles under the weight of his frustration. "Are you really so stubborn that you won't ask me to hold the flashlight? This is your plan? Fix the sink with unsteady light so you don't have to rely on me for the smallest thing?"

I secure the wrench where it needs to go and turn the fitting with my teeth gritted. "Fine!" I let the flashlight drop from between my legs so he can scoop it up.

"You're a real piece of work, you know that?" Rome shines the light on the pipe for me.

"Yeah, yeah. You break it, you bought it."

"Hilarious. How do I fix it?"

I glare at him to keep the hurt from shining through. "You make your peace with the fact that you might not be able to. Don't be a better person for me. Do it for you. Then you won't run out on the next girl who's stupid enough to fall for your charm and your raspberry cannoli."

Rome holds my gaze, digesting my advice because it's

the only path forward I have given him that hasn't sent him from my presence. "There will never be anyone else," he promises me. "Whether or not you return my affections is irrelevant. I am not the kind of man who needs to be in love. It's only you. Always you."

I don't doubt his faithfulness. That's not the issue. "Wrong," I counter. "It's only *you*. Always *you*. You got spooked and you ran, thinking only of yourself."

Rome closes his eyes, resting his hand atop my bare foot. "I can do better."

"Good for you." I fix my focus on the U-bend that is now dripping onto my tank top.

Rome looks at me with equal parts anger and agony. "You told me I had your heart."

"Funny thing, that. After you left and took it with you, I found that a heart is completely unnecessary. Keep it. Burn it. I don't care. I have no use for the dead weight any longer."

Rome lowers his head. It's odd to see him on his knees, so submissive. "You cannot possibly be this cynical."

"I am the Last Deadblood. I can be all sorts of things. The world is filled with possibility." I can't see the pipe to know if I am making any true headway. "Aim the flashlight a little to the right. That's left." I harrumph as Rome's help is proving less than helpful at first glimpse. "My right, my right."

"Sorry. You see that's dripping, yes?"

"So that's what that wetness is on my shirt," I reply glibly.

I do my best to focus on the task at hand, but Rome isn't going to make that easy. I can feel his breath on my shins as he kneels in front of my bent legs.

He is so close; my breathing syncopates. I shouldn't let his proximity affect me, but the lure Rome has on my senses is always there. Unrelenting, his body calls to mine, drawing me closer because that is the magnet he is to what is left of my soul.

I fight the urge to kick him square in the groin, which wouldn't be hard to do at all from this position. I hate that he is here.

I hate that he left.

I didn't want to deal with my feelings about his absence, but now that he's back, I have to. I shouldn't be drawn to him as I am for all the obvious reasons, but that doesn't stop my heart from wanting the devilish things it tries to convince me I cannot live without.

Rome leans his head under the sink to get a better look. He frowns at the pipe. "I can call a plumber if you don't want my help. The drip is hitting your shirt, little cannoli. Please. You know how I get when you don't let me help."

"Help and control are two sides of the same coin. I can do this just fine. The house was a bargain. It was bound to have a few kinks. It's nothing I'm not prepared to handle."

The house was thirty grand less than what I was aiming to pay for a place of my own. It was miraculous, really. It's a big plot of land, which is good for keeping people out of my private space so I can truly decompress.

I didn't even have to negotiate.

My wrench freezes on the pipe as what should have been obvious clicks into place. "You're the reason this house was such a deal." I close my eyes, wondering how it is that I didn't see it before. "I'm so stupid. You interfered. You had them lower their asking price."

Rome's silence says it all.

I should be angry. Part of me is at least indignant.

But that traitor part of me that still belongs to Rome longs to wrap my arms around his neck so I can whisper in his ear how grateful I am for his overreaching love.

Instead of choosing which reaction I should have, I put my effort into unscrewing the fitting on the pipe. I haven't used the sink all day, but when I finally pull the thing loose, I shriek at the unexpected deluge that dumps itself on my torso.

Rome slides me out from under the sink, chuckling at my plight as he shoves a bucket under the pipe to catch the rest. "Was that your plan?"

"Don't make jokes! Yuck! I'm dripping with sewage."

Rome helps me to stand, chuckling at the puddle of dirty water and grime that slides down my legs. He grabs up a hand towel and kneels before me, dabbing at my shins while I debate ripping off my clothes in the middle of the kitchen, so I don't have to track grossness through the house.

He reaches beneath the sink and fishes around, coming back with the root of the problem. "Egg shells. That's your culprit."

"Great. So I only have myself to blame. I'm the one who made eggs last."

Rome can't stop grinning, not even bothering to cover over his laughter. "Why don't you go wash up. I'll put this back together and clean up. It'll be like it never happened."

I take him up on his offer of help only because I am filthy, and a shower is the one thing in the world that sounds good right now.

But the moment I take a step toward the hallway, my security system chimes, letting me know someone entered my home.

I freeze, unsure who it could be. Orlando is in the West End, so it's not him. Declan is at work, so it's not him. Everyone else knocks and waits for me to let them in.

Rome puts down the towel and reaches for his gun. He presses his finger to his lips. Then he motions to the open door of the pantry, silently telling me that's where I should hide.

I don't like the idea of hiding from an intruder, but I don't argue. My feet are soundless as I slide my body into the pantry, waiting for Rome to close me inside. With his gun in his right hand, he thumbs my cheek with his left, letting me know that he will protect my home.

Even though I have made it my business to punish him well beyond what I should.

Even though we might never get back together.

Even though most likely the reason there is someone in my house is because they are after me, not him.

Without making a sound, I feel around in my pantry for anything that might prove useful in a gun fight.

My firearms aren't in the kitchen. I have a knife in my freezer, but that's hardly accessible from here.

I close my eyes and do what I can to think invisible thoughts. It's childish and ineffective, I'm sure, but it is my only course of action.

I picture Rome inching toward the intruder, gun at the ready. I hate that he is in this situation. I hate that he didn't stay gone, if only because it means he is here and in danger now.

I hate that I care this much about him still, and in fact might always feel the assault of any hit aimed his way.

My hand moves to my sopping chest, my palm flat over my heart, where I feel him most acutely.

Though I don't have a way to contact Orlando, that doesn't stop me from trying. I do my best attempt at calling him in my brain, attaching myself to our connection and putting probably too much faith in it.

Our link tells me when Orlando needs certain things.

It's not a telephone wire that allows me to deliver messages.

But that doesn't stop me from trying.

I pretend Orlando is standing right in front of me, looking down on my sewage-soaked form in that serious way he always has about him. Though my eyes are closed, my chin lifts while I pretend he is close enough to talk to.

Orlando, come home. Someone is in the house.

I wait for a beat, wondering if that did anything.

I am connected with Orlando, sure, but right now I want to be in sync with Rome. My breath is silent, but each inhale feels powerful, like I am trying to change my atmosphere with every expansion of my lungs.

Do I love Rome? Of course. Do I forgive him? No.

Does that latter point matter in this situation?

Not in the slightest.

An image of Rome floats in my mind's eye. I can picture him lurking through my house, searching for the criminal who dared breech my safe place.

An odd echoing pings in my chest.

Rome is afraid. I can tell even from here, in the dark and through the distance set in place between us. Rome is afraid not for himself, but for me.

My father gives out a warning when he's got his gun aimed at a person, but that's his police training. Rome doesn't believe in warnings. The shut door was the warning.

When a gun fires, I press my lips shut to stifle my scream. I can only hope that when I come out of the pantry, the man I shouldn't love isn't lying in a puddle of his own blood.

15

SUSPECT BULLET

Rome is standing in the center of my living room, which is no small relief. He is barking into his phone, his brows furrowed as he stands over the body of a man who is howling while holding his knee.

I don't recognize the man on the floor. He's got curly red hair with a bald patch on the back. He looks to be in his late forties, his freckles vivid against his pale skin while he grits his teeth through the pain of being shot in the knee.

When Rome catches sight of me in his periphery, he sends me a look of sheer exasperation. "You don't need to see this, tré-sur. Go back into the kitchen. I will handle it."

I bite down on my lower lip, ignoring his order. I should get far away from the threat of violence, but in this moment, all I care about is verifying with my own two eyes that no part of Rome has been harmed.

I flit to his side, unable to remain stoic when my heart is beating this erratically. I surprise us both when my arms go around him, anxiety flooding my system. Rome tells the person on the phone to get here now. Then he ends the call and slides his phone into his pocket.

With the gun trained on the intruder, Rome wraps his free arm around me, pressing my filthy body to his side. He kisses the top of my head, shushing my worries with his calm assurances. "It's okay, little cannoli. I will never let anyone take you ever again. You are safe, do you hear me?"

I burrow my face into the meat of his shoulder. "I don't care about me," I admit. "I was worried he shot you! Are you okay? Are you hurt?"

Rome's hand knows how to be gentle even in the roughest of circumstances. His thumb traces the curve of my hip, which I know is one of his favorite places on my body. "I have you in my arms. Even if I was seconds away from death, I would not be in any pain."

I should let go of him, but I'm not sure I am physically able to unfurl my fist from his white shirt.

Rome doesn't rush me. Though he just shot a man, his touch is gentle. He even goes so far as to sway slightly to rock my worries into a dull roar. How he can maim someone and then find enough stillness in his soul to settle mine is beyond me.

"Did he hurt you?" I whisper while the man on the

floor screams. He is bleeding all over my carpet, but his shrieks are mere background noise.

"He didn't lay a finger on me, tré-sur. Didn't I promise I would keep you safe?"

I blink up at Rome, overwhelmed by his beauty when he is this close. "But who keeps you safe?"

He stares into my eyes, drinking in my concern as if it is the one thing he has been struggling to survive without. If he kissed me right now, I'm not sure I would have the strength to pull away.

Rome's lips move closer to mine, his lashes fluttering shut as if being this close to me is an intoxicant he cannot steel himself against.

"Gross! What are you..." the criminal says of our obvious affection. Then his pain takes over. "My knee!" The man on the floor screams, interrupting our haze.

I jerk away from Rome, blinking myself out of the fog of infatuation just long enough to realize this is hardly the time to reconnect. I stand one whole foot away from him, breaking our embrace so I can think clearer. "I'll call the sheriff."

"No need. Orlando is on his way."

I raise my brow at Rome. "Hello, Orlando's not a cop."

"Hello," Rome mocks me, "a cop isn't going to handle this. We are."

"What?"

Rome motions to the man on the floor. "I will handle this. I'm not going to risk this guy paying a minimal sentence for what he's done. That's only going to fuel him more when he gets out. Orlando and I will deal with it. We can extract more information from him than your father legally can, anyway."

I chew on my lower lip. I don't know what to say to that, other than that it's a total breech of the law.

And completely expected that this is how Rome would choose to deal with it.

"The sheriff should know who is aiming for me," I argue.

"I'll share the information with your father once I have it."

I rub the nape of my neck. "That's a fair enough compromise, I guess."

Rome holds my gaze. "I don't want you to worry about this, Coletta. This man will never come for you again."

The intruder whimpers because he knows as well as I do that his hours are numbered.

The man's gun is a few feet away from where he writhes on the floor. Just in case, I flit over to him and pick up the weapon, emptying the cartridge and taking out the bullet that's in the chamber.

I've loaded enough guns—my own and others—to know how a bullet should feel in your palm. My stomach drops when the thing in my hand leaves a slick trail across the inside of my hand.

My heart pounds as a whole new revelation opens itself to me. "Rome," I whisper, but there's no sound behind the rasp. I mouth his name over and over, unable to force my horror to make sense.

I'm wrong. I have to be wrong. This can't be what my eyes are telling me.

I stand in the center of the living room, staring at the slick bullet, too scared to speak until Orlando barrels in through the front door with his gun at the ready.

Once he assesses the situation and rules that we are not in danger anymore, he takes in my pallor. "Coco, what happened?"

Rome explains the situation from start to finish, but that doesn't alleviate Orlando's concern. He moves to my side, but when he approaches, I back away with a shriek, suddenly finding my volume. "No! Stay back!"

Orlando jerks as if I have slapped him. He holds his hands up, as if he assumes he is the one of which I am afraid.

That could never be the case. Orlando is my big sweetie pie.

I close my hand around the bullet, fear rounding my eyes. "This attack wasn't meant for me," I whisper to the men I love. When I unfurl my fingers, a red streak across my palm displays itself to the room. "The bullet was dipped in blood. My blood, I'm guessing."

Rome freezes while Orlando takes another step back.

"He wasn't after me," I tell them, scared that this is what my world has come to. My gaze slowly lifts from the sticky bullet to the men standing in my living room. "It was meant to kill one of you."

16

MY DATE

Though I have precious little free time, when Declan tells me he wants to go see a truly ridiculous-looking horror movie with me next week, my schedule suddenly opens up. After an entire week of Rome being nothing short of the perfect man, I need my brother to shake me out of this haze of need I am rapidly falling into.

"You should come," I tell Orlando as I shove a raspberry cannoli in my mouth. It's my third one this morning, but I have no intention of slowing down. Rome made them from scratch in this very kitchen last night while I worked. Rome, Orlando and I talked over what he thought we should tackle next in Mayfield while Rome cooked for us.

We haven't spoken of the fact that someone stole my blood and used it to try and murder one of them. We still don't know which of them the fatal bullet was meant to take out; the intruder died before he came clean about all he knew.

We don't know his intended target.

We don't know if he was working alone.

We don't know who told him one of the Valentino men would be inside my house.

We don't know anything, other than that my blood was stolen and used by a member of the revolution named Calvin. The guys won't give me his last name. They seem to be united in their quest to keep this incident from imprinting itself in my brain. They must think that if they can convince me that they are not worried someone is aiming my blood their way trying to murder one of the men I love, then I will magically forget the dire realities of my world.

It's not their worst plan.

Orlando snorts at my movie suggestion. "I'll go, but only to keep an eye on the exits. Your taste in movies is appalling."

I guffaw but don't argue further.

Rome sips his morning espresso from his stool at the kitchen counter while he reads the paper, looking every bit the man of my house with his cool demeanor. "You have your meeting with Nico this morning. Are you still sure that's a good idea?"

I force a light laugh. "It's a great idea. I'm proud of myself for being so brilliant in my vindictiveness. Nico will loathe being so close to me, making friendly chitchat over tea. But maybe Nico will give me some information about this Calvin fellow and why he broke into my house, intent on killing one of you."

Neither of them acknowledges I spoke.

I sip my tea while I stand at the counter, deciding to push further into the wound they are both pretending doesn't exist. "Maybe Nico will know how Calvin got his hands on my blood, or how he knew one of you two would be in my house. Nico will know why Calvin broke into my house to get to you instead of hunting you down in the West End."

Rome keeps his eyes on his paper. "Orlando, when you go to the movie with Coletta and Declan, can you pick me up some red vines? It's been a while since I've had those. I can share a few with Nico, who knows to keep his mouth shut about things that have already been taken care of."

Orlando nods once. "Yup."

I scowl through my next bite of raspberry cannoli. "I hate it when you two team up. I deserve to know who is coming for me."

Rome still does not look up from his paper. "No one is coming for you, little cannoli. A bullet soaked in Dead-blood is coming for us, and we have it handled."

I steel against his reasoning. "A bullet meant for either of you is just as good as it being aimed at me."

The corner of Rome's mouth quirks. "I love you, too."

I splutter a non-response, then shove the rest of the cannoli in my mouth to give myself a good excuse for not having a smart remark at the ready.

My phone rings, and I answer without thinking of how full my mouth is. "Hu-mmo?" I grab for my teacup to clear my mouth, but Orlando slides it out of reach with a mischievous grin.

Governor Ingrid Mason's cheery yet confident voice sobers me. "Hello, Madam Deadblood. Is this a good time?"

I swat at Orlando as I make every effort to swallow. "Of course, Governor Mason. What can I do for you?"

"Such a good attitude. I wanted to congratulate you on our win last week. That's a big step forward."

Orlando gives me back my teacup once he realizes this is an important phone call.

I take a long drink before I can answer. "It sure is. We couldn't have pushed it through without your help."

"I think we make a good team. Speaking of teamwork, I have a dinner I'm hosting at the mansion next week. I know it's short notice, but might you and your gentleman friend be available to attend?"

My movements still. "Why?" I don't say it with attitude, but more wondering why on earth she would invite a vampire to her table. I am viciously protective of the Valentino family, and don't want Orlando to have to suffer through a dinner where he would not be welcome.

"Because you both have to eat, and I have a fantastic caterer."

"How about you and I don't bullshit each other," I suggest, lowering all pretense of formality. If we do this, I want all the cards out on the table. I actually admire the governor, and don't want to dance around the issues with her.

The governor sighs. "That is definitely a good policy, and one I don't often adhere to. But in our case, perhaps shooting straight is the best way forward. I want you and your vampire gentleman to come because it means something to have a vampire at the table. No other public servants would dare attempt something so audacious. If we are going to show the world that vampires are civil, then this is necessary. I'm sure Rome Valentino would rather eat glass than dine with a bunch of stuck-up officials, but if he could take one for the team, it might open people's eyes, thus opening opportunities for other vampires to be invited to more tables."

My reply comes out slow as the two men in the room freeze. "You want Rome to come because..."

"Because the picture of the two of you that circulated on the internet did its job of convincing the world that he is dating the Last Deadblood. I want Mayfield to lead the way for vampire rights, instead of always lagging behind."

I press my lips together. "I see." My mouth tightens. "Sorry, but it's a no-go. Your mansion is in the East End.

Vampires aren't allowed there, thanks to the city's outdated law."

The governor seems to have anticipated my response. "I am prepared to push through a motion in the morning to redact that law, if all goes well."

I pause, unable to believe my good luck. "Are you serious?" Then I think through her phrasing. "You mean, you'll push through the necessary change if I agree to bring Rome to your house?"

A brief pause comes before her reply. "That's correct. All little something I want for a big something you want."

I chew on my lower lip.

Rome is motionless in his stool at the kitchen counter beside Orlando. He is staring so intently at me that I swear, I can feel the heat of his gaze on my face.

I don't want it to be this easy. I don't want Rome to step into the role of boyfriend because the governor, of all people, is pushing us together.

But lifting the ban of vampires in the East End is too big a promise to pass on.

I pinch the bridge of my nose. "Can you hold, please?" I don't wait for her answer before I put her on mute. I don't want her to hear my obvious fretting. "Did you two catch all that?"

Orlando nods. "Good that she's taking a step like this. Being invited to a dinner for policymakers isn't something that's ever happened to a vampire. I like that she's taking a risk, instead of it always being us pushing things forward. This is a good thing."

That's not my issue, and he knows it. He's playing dumb so I have to say it aloud and make it all awkward. "She thinks the picture of the two of us Declan took was Rome and me, not you and me. I know that's what the papers have largely been spreading around, but I didn't realize it was gospel fact."

Orlando fights with his smirk. "I'll have to tell Declan he did a good job taking that picture. I was hoping they would see the Valentino family ring and draw their own conclusions."

I glower at him. "I'm not ready to be pushed into anything."

Rome's voice is quiet. "I can remember it's a charade and not read into it."

I shoot him a wry look. "I sincerely hope you enjoyed that lie."

Rome winks at me, suddenly filled with a resurgence of the cockiness that seemed to have left him weeks ago. "I certainly did, my little cannoli. Tell the governor I'll be there, dressed in my finest and happy to play the role of the man on your arm. She can prepare herself for us to parade up and down the streets of the East End after that, holding hands to the shock and horror of the upscale East End neighbors."

Ever since the almost-kiss that occurred over Calvin's

bloody body, I have been giving Rome a wide berth, making sure to keep an arm's length of space between us at all times. I'm not sure I am ready to spend an evening with Rome by my side.

I am not strong enough to keep my lips from his. The draw to be near him is so strong that I put my chair in front of my bedroom door last night to keep myself from going to him in the dark.

I put the phone to my cheek and mull through my options. "Governor Mason? If you can make room for both Orlando and Rome Valentino to be my guests at your dinner, then we will be there."

I stare inquisitively at Orlando, who rolls his eyes at my cowardice.

The governor's voice is filled with elation. "Wonderful! Black tie. Press always covers these things."

Orlando mouths something that I repeat to the governor. "Can I get a list of those who will be in attendance?" I scrunch my brows at Orlando, wondering why he wants me to ask such an impertinent thing.

"That can be arranged."

When we end the call, Orlando whistles at the change our morning has taken. "Might have to break out the good suit for this thing."

Rome chuckles, his eyes still on his newspaper. "So you need a chaperone to go on a date with me now? Are you afraid you'll make a move on me, so you need Orlando to supervise?"

Yes.

"No," I spout petulantly, my cheeks pinking because Rome is good at spotting my obvious lies.

Rome shakes his head while he laughs at me, so I change the subject, addressing Orlando instead. "Why do we need a list of the governor's guests?"

Orlando takes another sip of his coffee in lieu of answering. "Reasons. When are you planning on going to the movie with Declan?"

I rattle off the time and date as I set my dishes in the sink.

"I can't make it." Orlando finishes his coffee. "I also don't want to make it. I've seen your taste in movies. I was planning on taking Nico on a raid that night. Want to place bets on whose night is more filled with gratuitous violence?" His brows dance comically.

"Hello, my movie is called *Silent Grandma*. You know it's going to be brutal. It's about a grandmother who's lost her mind, but she sends out her spirit to murder the people who have wronged her... Or have they?" My eyebrows to dance with mischief to match his.

Orlando chuckles at our easy back and forth as he stands. "Good for you for having a little fun. You've been nonstop all week. I was beginning to forget what your face looks like when it's not obscured by your computer."

I link my fingers and spread them wide under my chin, blinking up innocently at Orlando. "This face?"

"That's the one. All sweetness and sin."

I press my lips together at what I am pretty sure passes for a compliment from Orlando. We walk together to the living room, gathering up all we need for the day.

"Oh," I tell him as I reach for my coat. "I forgot to tell you that your phone rang while you were in the shower. Nico."

Orlando's levity dies. "He gets antsy, wanting to start early when we're about to go on raids. I keep telling him these sorts of things need moonlight, but whatever. One day, he'll learn."

"You keep telling yourself that." I reach up and pinch his cheek. "My big sweetie pie. Such a sweet little optimist."

Orlando rubs the slight sting off his face. "I think that's the first time anyone has ever called me that."

Rome's form catches my eye from the entryway of the living room. "You need a third for your movie?"

Orlando slides on his suit jacket. "She does. I was thinking of going on another raid that night without you. Nico needs to learn to fall in line without you there. This should be a pretty simple one."

Rome nods. "Sounds good. I haven't seen Declan in a while. Wouldn't mind that."

I glower at Orlando, but he pretends not to see it. He

knows I am this close to caving. It's hard to be around Rome without envisioning my fingers coiled in his hair.

Orlando grabs his keys. "Have fun, kids. I'll be out late, so don't wait up for me."

I narrow one eye at Orlando's blatant setup. He's been doing that all week, calling after Rome gets to the house to tell me he's running late.

Orlando grins at me, no doubt loving that we're all getting what we want out of his subterfuge.

But it's too soon. I don't want to get back together with Rome if he's going to split again once things get real.

"Tell me about the raid," I demand, trying to keep my tone light and conversational. Orlando's collar is flipped up, so I tuck it down. I straighten his suit because it matters to me if he leaves disheveled. "You haven't done one in a while."

Orlando checks his phone while he talks. "Nothing big. Just a few halluci-dens getting a little too full. Nico saw an underaged kid going in there earlier this week. It's time to intervene."

I grimace, worry wrinkling my brow. "I don't like this. Maybe the sheriff should be involved."

Orlando boops my nose, smirking at our close proximity. "If he wanted to be, he would. This is our people, our side of the city, so we will handle it. That's how things work, Coco."

Rome moves further into the living room. "Even if the

sheriff did involve himself, it doesn't send a strong enough message. Our people need to respect us when we set down the law that there will be no more halluci-blend being dealt in the West End."

Orlando opens the front door, but before he leaves, he kisses my cheek.

It's a small thing. For most people, it's nothing of note. But Orlando doesn't hand out small affections like party favors.

Warmth spreads across my face from the point of contact, heating my insides like a cozy fire on a cold day.

Rome watches the exchange but says nothing, which, as it turns out, is the exact right thing to say.

17

THE GOVERNOR'S DINNER

I haven't worn a gown in quite some time, and when I did, it certainly wasn't a designer dress from Ming Lu. The deep blue material cascades over my hips like a waterfall as I walk with Rome and Orlando into the governor's mansion.

The place is lavish yet tasteful, with dark wood and emerald details in the gold fixtures. "Beautiful," I marvel. "Reminds me of your home."

Rome's gait has been stiff since we got in the car to come here, but he manages an airy laugh at my observation. "Ours isn't nearly this big."

"My memories of the Valentino mansion are from when I was like, three feet tall. Everything was huge and impressive back then."

He keeps my hand wrapped in the crook of his elbow. Though he appears cool and in control in his suit with his shoes shined, I can feel his jumping pulse through his ribcage. "Do me a favor and stay by my side tonight, okay? I don't like the feel of this place."

I don't argue, knowing this is well outside a vampire's comfort zone. Orlando and Rome are the first vampires to ever step inside the governor's mansion, which I am sure might carry the flavor of a setup to them.

I cling tighter to reassure him. "We don't have to do this. Say the word and we go home."

Rome swallows hard, expressing his uncertainty only to me. "No. This is important. This is a moment." Determination chases away his insecurity, or at least masks it well enough for us to put one foot in front of the other. "I belong here."

I straighten on his arm. "Yes, you do. We belong where we put ourselves."

Rome glances down at me, forcing lightness into his countenance. "This is our first public date, you realize. You might only be doing this for the cause of equal rights, but for me, it's our first date."

At that moment, it hits me. That is exactly what we are doing. This is the date we always wanted when we were sneaking around at our beach, desperate to be together but afraid of being seen.

How I wish this opportunity had come when we were together, and not in this limbo of distrust.

Although, maybe this is our first date. Not the first date

we should have had (though it is that), but the first date of us starting anew.

Am I ready for such a giant leap?

Will Rome leave all over again the moment things get real?

I chew on my lower lip as butterflies swarm in my belly. The suit, the dress, and the beautiful twilight all push me over the edge without any semblance of a safety net. Before I can think through my decision, I am already speaking it aloud. "Then let's enjoy ourselves. We're always playing strategy with everyone. Tonight, could we actually have a first date?" I blink up at him, worried I'm not being clear. "Could this be real?"

Rome stops and turns to me on the front porch, where we wait for Orlando to join us after parking the car. His eyes fix on me with a seriousness that belies the confident cool he was trying to project mere seconds ago. "Is that what you want? Do you forgive me for leaving? You're really willing to give us another chance?"

"Is it fair that I don't know the answers to any of those questions?" My body doesn't back away from his, but leans in so I can tentatively touch the chest muscle I have been missing. "I want to enjoy tonight. I never thought we would be able to have this. A real date in public, where we don't have to pretend we don't care about each other."

Though we aren't exactly alone, given that people are

coming up the walk to go to the party, Rome thumbs my lips. "Then this is our first date."

We never had one of those, unless I count the trips to the beach done in secret. But this is a date in public, complete with all the uncertainties and nerves that go into making a first date a memorable risk.

Is betting on Rome worth the risk of losing what scraps I have saved of my heart?

I don't know. But I am certain that if I don't take this leap, I will always wonder if I could forgive, if I could have, if we could love.

I am attuned to the sound of cell phones taking pictures, and wince when I hear one coming from behind us. But this time a news crew jumps out of a minivan and jogs toward us with purpose.

"Here we go," I warn Rome.

A microphone is shoved in my face by a man who looks like he often disguises his ambition with a forceful smile, showing off his whitened, show biz-ready set of teeth. "Madam Deadblood, Peter Breggs with Channel Eleven. What a nice change to have you added to the list of guests at Governor Mason's dinner. Tell us about your date this evening."

I lift my nose in the air, drawing authority to me as if I am a witch with a spell up my sleeve. "I'm sure you are not so removed from Mayfield that you don't know who Rome Valentino is," I tell the man flippantly.

"Yes, but we want to know more. How did this happen? Why? Is the world safer, now that you're taking up with a vampire? Does this ensure that you are, in fact, the Last Deadblood? Since vampires and humans can't procreate, are our worries put to bed now?"

I am accustomed to all sorts of caustic questions being shouted at me because reporters often forget I am also a person. But this is so far over the line, I cannot fathom how I am supposed to conjure up a cool response.

Rome steps in, offering his hand to the man to shake. He smiles, but there is no joy in the expression; it is an excuse to intimidate the man by showing off his fangs. "Are you worried about who my lovely girlfriend is having sex with? Is that truly a thing that keeps you up at night, Peter? You see a beautiful woman dressed for a fine evening out, and you automatically have to know who's in her bed and whether or not she is getting pregnant tonight?" He clucks his tongue at the reporter. "And they call vampires savage."

Calling me his girlfriend is a bit of a reach, but I'm glad Rome takes control of the conversation so I can recover my bearings.

To his credit, Peter Breggs only grimaces, but he doesn't lose his tenacity. "Your legacy affects us all, Madam Deadblood. Are the vampires in danger from your offspring, or will the damage die with you?" Then he turns to Rome before I can do more than gape at him. "This is your first time in the East End since the territory ban was lifted. Tell me how you like the East End, Mister Valentino."

Rome narrows his eye at the reporter. "I can see where my tax dollars are going—into beautifying the East End only."

The reporter laughs, of all things.

Gross.

Peter Breggs then turns his attention back to me. "Still waiting on your answer, Madam Deadblood. Are the vampires going to have more generations of terror, or are you going to remain celibate for the greater good?"

I swallow hard, reminding myself that if his cameraman gets a picture of me shoving the caustic reporter off the porch, that will not help my cause. "Have a lovely evening. Enjoy daydreaming about my uterus." I turn and march into the mansion, where you can get inside by invite only. "I know we were supposed to wait for Orlando outside, but if I stay on that porch a second longer, I'm going to make front page news tomorrow."

"I think you'll be front page no matter what." Rome motions between us. "This is a big deal."

I shake my head, straightening my shoulders. "It's normal," I tell myself. "Whenever I'm on a date, everyone has to know. There's always cameras. There is always a story done on the guy. It's fine."

Rome scowls. "You are not a zoo animal. I can't believe

he talked to you like that. I mean, I guess I knew it happened, but to be on your arm when it did was intense."

"Believe me, if my date were anyone else, he would be treated to the same thing."

"I know. I've read the profiles on your other dates in the papers. I just didn't realize it would feel so intrusive. How are we supposed to enjoy ourselves if everything we do is being photographed?"

How, indeed. Maybe this was a bad idea.

Rome takes in a deep breath, as if we just landed a narrow escape. "The governor won't let the reporters inside. This dinner is going to be filled with people who are sick of being photographed and speculated over. We got in the door. The hard part is over."

"If you say so."

18

LACEY'S LOOSE LIPS

I am not the best date in the world, but I am determined to try. This is our chance to have what we wanted for so many months. I will not shy away and squander the opportunity now.

We stand just inside the door, our hearts pounding until Orlando joins us, giving us a third member of our awkward party to focus on so we don't say something stupid to each other and ruin the night.

Orlando's hand on the small of my back is reassuring as he walks on my other side, caging in my body with his as we move further into the mansion. He doesn't give his name to the greeter just inside the foyer, but stares the man down until he hurriedly checks our names off the list.

When Orlando falls back to walk behind us, Rome's arm affixes itself around my hips. It doesn't remove itself until we are ushered into the great hall, where there are tall tables for champagne and gilded sconces giving off a romantic glow under the mural painted across the ceiling. The room is huge with the roof being several stories above, giving the impression that this mansion is hundreds of years old, fit for the kings of the past and coopted by the ill-fitted rulers of today.

I smile unconvincingly at seven people as they introduce themselves to me. The great hall is breathtaking. The string quartet plays in the corner to the dozens milling about. They each have the look of steeling themselves before they greet us, braving being near Rome to shake the hand of the Last Deadblood.

Most everyone else gives us a wide berth after a brief introduction, talking in pockets with covert glances aimed our way. The three of us ignore the waiters circling the room with trays of hors d'oeuvres. I couldn't eat if I was starving, which I'm not. I am too nervous, knowing that everything we do is scrutinized, even in this setting.

The governor enters the great hall. It looks like it might have been used as a ballroom, back when balls were things that were thrown by public figures. Ingrid Mason smiles and makes her way around the room with her assistant on her heels—a woman in her late twenties who whispers the names of people in her boss' ear before each interaction. The woman looks a little nervous, but determined to be the best assistant ever. Her movements are sharp and her steps quick as she scampers along behind the governor in her simple black dress and heels.

When the governor gets to us, she shakes my hand with both of hers, and then kisses both my cheeks. "Lovely, Madam Deadblood. Thank you for coming."

"Of course."

Then she does something I can tell no one is expecting. She reaches out and offers to shake Rome's hand—a thing no one here has deigned to do. "And thank you for escorting her, Mister Valentino." When he grasps her hand briefly, she meets his eyes with interest. "Truly."

Rome dips his head to her. "I should be thanking you. This is our first date. I am determined to enjoy it."

The governor winks at us. "Well played. Good. Convincing everyone this is real is the way to pave a brighter future where vampires and humans are more equal."

Of course, what she doesn't realize is that we actually are together. Or mostly together. Or were together.

I don't know which way is up anymore. It's this dress. Ming Lu didn't hold back. The pale blue gown brushes my toes while a complicated lattice laces up my back, magically holding my breasts aloft. While my cleavage is in no danger of spilling out, it is quite clear that I am not afraid of my body.

There are more pressing things to fear.

I catch the eye of the governor's assistant. "May I steal your friend, here?"

"Who, Lacey?"

I nod. "Sure. No one seems to want to talk with us, but perhaps someone on your staff won't be as jittery around us." I motion around the room. "As it is, everyone here is afraid to get near us for more than a few seconds. If you want my guests' presence normalized at your event, then you have to do more than just let us in the door."

The governor mulls over my suggestion for a beat and then nods. "Of course. Lacey, see to it that Madam Deadblood gets anything she requires."

That's not exactly what I asked for, but whatever. At least if Lacey is near us, we won't look like lepers, hanging on the periphery of the party.

Plus, she is the only person here who looks near my age.

"Yes, ma'am."

The governor moves onto the next group of people, greeting them with a pleasant smile.

I loop my free arm through Lacey's, forcing her to be my best friend for the night. "How much do you want to bet the governor won't greet a single person by name, now that you're with me?"

Lacey lets loose a nervous snicker. "She is terrible with names. I don't mind helping, but at some point, she needs to actually learn the names of the spouses she invites to her parties."

"It's sink or swim time, it looks like."

We watch while the governor greets the Secretary Treasurer by name but smiles blandly at his wife, offering a perfunctory hello.

"This will be fun. At least we won't be the only ones flustered at this event."

Lacey motions to the cluster of people in the corner. "Oh, everyone is on edge."

"Should I apologize for that?" I have no intention to, but I might as well call attention to the elephant in the room.

"They're not used to seeing you in person. They read about you, but eating with you is a whole other thing. Rumors about the way you handed Mayor Stapleton's ass to him have circulated." Her eyes widen as she cuffs her hand over her mouth "I just swore in front of the Last Deadblood!"

I chuckle at Lacey's fretting. "Better than swearing at me."

She glances around and then casts me a devious grin. "Did you really make Mayor Stapleton cry?"

I laugh at the rumor. "Do men generally cry when they wet themselves?"

Lacey and Rome share a chortle, then look at each other after sharing in the same joke. Lacey dips her head in his direction. "Mister Valentino, it's good to have you here."

Rome regards her coolly. "Is it? Huh."

Lacey bobs her head, still with that look of eagerness about her that no doubt makes her a fantastic assistant. "Oh, yes. The governor is ready to make a statement."

Rome raises an eyebrow at her. "And what statement is that? That vampires can be kept out of businesses, but because we're invited to the mansion, it's all water under the bridge?"

Lacey's eyes widen. "Not at all. The statement is that she is moving in that direction, whether the rest of the world is ready or not."

When it is clear Rome is not impressed, Lacey shuts her mouth.

But I am still glad I insisted Lacey stay by my side. She points out several sympathizers to our cause of equality and tells us who is on the fence. Listening to her rattle on is invaluable because it shows me where I need to aim my focus.

"What about that group over there?" I ask, nodding toward a cluster of men who are speaking in hushed tones over brandy. "I don't recognize most of them, except the state senator."

Lacey's expression closes off. "You don't want to meet them, and they don't want to meet you." She glances behind her to Orlando. "You're the one to tell that, right? You're the bodyguard."

Orlando doesn't speak. He got the list of attendees prior to the party, so he no doubt did enough digging to have positioned us on the opposite side of the ballroom from the group most hostile to us.

Gotta love him.

Orlando is a shadow behind me, listening but not speaking and not wanting any sort of attention or communication. I know him well enough to guess that he is searching Lacey's body language to see if she's got any sort of weapon on her.

I lean in, keeping my expression pleasant enough so it doesn't look like we are conspiring. "I know Senator Collins always votes for vampires to fix the West End themselves. He's always trying to limit their rights. Who are the people with him?"

Lacey's lips press together. "I'm sure they wouldn't want me telling you who they are. They're the senator's guests, as far as we are concerned." She fixes her eyes on mine. I can tell she is forcing herself to step out into the unknown with her next statement. "The men he brought are part of the revolution."

My eyes widen. "What? Are you serious? How do you even know that?"

Lacey motions to the guards at the exits. "You have your

security? The governor has hers. We don't know how far the revolution goes. Really, we only suspect them, but there's enough evidence to suggest Senator Collins is in contact with the revolution, and travels with them to things like this." She puts her hand on mine. "You're here to draw them out so they show their true colors. Did you not know that?"

Rome stiffens. "You invited us here so we could be bait? You wanted them to show themselves?" He speaks through gritted teeth. "Don't you understand how dangerous that is? They could have a plan to abduct her! If they do that, the entire vampire people are in danger."

Lacey's neck shrinks. "We took that into consideration. There is far more security here than you realize. You are perfectly safe. We needed this because the revolution is getting antsy. The Sheriff of Mayfield reported more threats aimed your way in the form of letters, Madam Deadblood. We wanted to bring the stains of humanity to the surface, so we could get them off the streets. Then you're safer."

Orlando touches my hip from behind. "We're leaving. This wasn't the plan."

I quite agree, but Rome cements his feet to the floor. "No. They have us where they want us. If we leave now, we're no safer. Let's take advantage of the extra security and play the game." His arm around my hips draws me closer. "The governor wants a show? Let's give her one she'll never forget. Watch how angry the revolutionaries get when I do this." He runs his finger down my cheek, looking at me as if I am the only woman who has ever caught his eye.

As if he has stepped his foot on a bomb, the other end of the room erupts in an angry exchange, watching our love from afar and no doubt planning on how best to take me out for betraying our race so blatantly.

Rome folds his fingers through mine, uniting us because in this moment, I am more vampire than human. "Care to dance?" he asks me, looking very much like the most dashing piece of danger I could ever lay eyes on.

There is violin music, but this hardly seems the occasion for dancing. But just because it's not being done doesn't mean we can't set precedent.

As usual.

I take his offer with little more than trepidation fueling my steps. If we didn't stand out before, we surely will now.

My heart is pounding as Rome takes the lead, his arm coiling more firmly around my hips. Though his smile is tight, his gait is loose enough to lead. It's a good thing, because I cannot recall ever dancing with a man who wasn't Declan.

Fear leaps onto my face. "I don't know how to dance!" I whisper, tense and terrified.

It's as if my anxiety triggers confidence in him. He manages a smile for me, feigning ease in the middle of immense pressure. "I can fix that." He marries his hips to mine, moving us in a slow rhythm that matches the music as if it was made for us. "Check the exits over my shoulder. I watch your back, you watch mine. That's how we work."

That *is* how we function. I've missed being able to trust that he would be there to count on.

The urge to check over my shoulder for the revolutionaries is strong, but I take a leap of faith in Rome—in us—and keep my eyes on my mark.

I watch his back while he guards mine, the two of us turning all eyes to us because not only are we the only ones dancing, but we radiate the magic borne of our making.

"There we are," Rome says with relief so pure it almost looks like pain. "I missed us."

So did I. But now that we have found the best parts of each other, I can only hope we will get out of this party in one piece.

Rome touches my cheek, studying our connection with wonder that something so precious could be real. His blue eyes burn away the damaged parts of me as only the best smolders can do.

We are playing with fire, but when Rome looks at me like that, I'm not sure I can do anything but stand here and burn for him.

19

DANCING WITH THE SENATOR

Though I am sure dancing wasn't on the itinerary for the night, several others join us on the ballroom floor. We may have come with our positions and agendas in mind, but all of that is long forgotten now. Our stuffy and cool demeanors are drowned by the sound of the violins.

So enraptured in the moment am I that I startle when someone taps me on the shoulder. "Madam Deadblood," says a man I don't know. I feel like maybe I've seen him on TV in political debates. "May I cut in?"

I look to Rome, who steps back with a nod. I expect him to move to the side, but we are both surprised when the governor herself asks him for a dance.

It's a big deal—a human dancing with a vampire. And in public, no less. The governor is making a choice, a statement we cannot ignore.

The vampires are welcome here. They will not be treated as second-class citizens anymore.

I barely pay attention to the pleasant chatter the politician offers as he turns me slowly, his posture erect. Like everyone else, I am enraptured by the sight of Rome making history with a cool expression on his face, as if he breaks the social norms on the daily without thought for the consequences.

I wish I didn't love him so wholly. If only I could fend off the swelling of my heart by putting a cage of distrust around it. But I fear that even after our falling out, there will be part of me that will never be able to look away from this incredible man.

When the song turns, another state official takes my hand. On the song after that, I find myself in the arms of the state senator whom Lacey told us is affiliated with the revolutionaries.

My spine stiffens and I lose my step often, but Senator Collins turns me without commenting on my sudden lack of elegance. He is wearing several gold rings, his suit crisp and his pocket square starched. His hair is so blond, it's nearly white. The crinkles around his eyes place his age at around fifty or so. He stares down at me with a tight expression that could pass for a smile in only the most dire of circumstances.

Senator Collins' posture is perfectly erect as he looks down his nose at me with an appraising menace to his gaze. "I heard the rumor that you would be here tonight, but I'll admit, I thought it a ruse to get us all to come to the governor's party. Yet here you are."

I blink up at him. "Here I am. Senator Collins, right? I didn't realize there were so many politicians. The ballroom is nearly full."

He sniffs dismissively at the onlookers as he holds his arms tight so I am not lost in the steps of the dance. "These events never draw this many. It's you we were hoping to see. Having you hidden away overseas made us speculate all the more what path you might take if you ever came back." He twirls me slowly and then brings me back. "I see you've decided to take up in your mother's footsteps, Youngblood. I didn't think you lacked caution to that extent. Reckless girl, indeed."

I don't know if he is warning me of the dangers of taking up my mother's mantle, or if he is merely making an observation.

This guy is slippery. I don't like not knowing a person's intentions.

"Did you know my mother well?" I ask him, trying to be conversational while I pray for the song to end.

The corner of his mouth crooks. "No one knew her. She was an enigma. A force of nature. The world changed because she demanded it so. Mayor Stapleton seems to have handed over that same weight of power to you." He narrows an eye at me. "I would caution you not to take errant steps with the world watching so closely. Dating a vampire? That's a scandal not even your mother would tolerate."

Finally. Now that he's laid his cards on the table, I know what I am working with.

"You seem to care an awful lot about who I'm dating, Senator. I hardly think my love life should be your top concern. I would guess you should be more worried about associating yourself with the revolutionaries over there than caring who I spend my free time with. Though, perhaps when people get insecure about their own choices, they distract themselves by picking at others."

My blatant scold raises his eyebrows. "Are you lecturing me? Aren't you twenty-five years old?"

"I am. And you're old enough to know better than to dip your toe into that pool." I jerk my chin toward the company he kept before he joined me on the dance floor.

A sharpness narrows his gaze. "How much do you want to bet that things go south for you before they ever crumble for me? You could lavish the entire world with jewels, but all they would see is the danger of your company and the risk to their one sure weapon." He turns me again and slowly pulls me back. "Me, on the other hand, all I'm doing is shaking hands with the people who will set things right if they go too far off course. People are glad the revolutionaries exist, because they will do the things the public wants to achieve but can't risk without looking uncivilized."

I step away when it dawns on me that I don't have to dance with anyone I don't want to, and I really don't want to be anywhere near this guy.

I put several feet between us. My stance is ready for a fight. My voice is prepared to put him in his place. "If that's how you see the people you serve, then I feel sorry for you and them. If you can't do better than this, then I think your time in office might be over."

He postures, suddenly looking much taller. "Is that a threat?"

"It's advice. My mother was patient; I am not."

"Apologies, Youngblood." The senator brushes past me after a quick bob of his head.

My lips purse when I feel a tiny scrap along the outside of my forearm.

Jerk snagged my skin with one of his gawdy rings.

My instinct to stand my ground despite the onlookers takes me over. My arm snaps out and catches his wrist, my eyes widening when I see one of his rings isn't a simple piece of jewelry at all.

I gasp as I take in his offending finger. My heart skips a beat when I realize he drew blood. Not much, but enough to kill the man I love if that was his intent.

The red jewel on his gold ring is flipped up on a tiny

hinge, exposing a short needle lurking beneath. The tip is smeared with fresh crimson.

"What did you do?" I whisper, scandalized that he isn't just associated with the revolutionaries, but he is one of them. "This ring. You wore it to take my blood!" I watch in horror as he flips the ruby on his ring back down, covering over the cavity where he collected a drop of my blood.

"I don't know what you mean," he tries to lie, as if that will erase the proof in plain sight.

"You think I am my mother's daughter?" I hiss, shaking my head as venom pools in my veins. "I am also my father's daughter, and I will see you locked up for this."

Senator Collins leans in, whispering with the fierceness of a man who will never see that he is wrong. "You crossed the line. It's my job to make sure humanity doesn't pay for it."

As if vampires are the monsters. As if when he looks in the mirror, he doesn't see that the true source of danger is staring him in the face.

"Orlando!" I shout, startling several people and drawing my most trusted guard toward me. I hold out my hand to stop his progression. "Get Rome out of here. Senator Collins stole my blood!"

Politicians and their dates whisper and point, scandalized but doing nothing to protect the vampires in the room.

The senator was right, I realize with sadness. The

people here don't care about making the world better. They haven't cracked down on the revolutionaries because the rogue group does the dirty work they won't admit to wanting to be part of.

The senator chuckles toward the onlookers as if I am a mere hysterical woman fretting over a broken fingernail. "Such drama. You scratched yourself while we were dancing. Come. Let's get you a band-aid."

As if I am five years old and my scrapes have no dire consequence.

When the senator grabs my wrist to try and direct me off the center of the dance floor, fury flares up in me. I will not be escorted anywhere by a revolutionary. I will not go anywhere with the man who wants to kill the people I love.

My fist rears back and flings with purpose, clocking Senator Collins clear across the jaw.

Now people react. Of course they do. How dare anyone hurt their precious senator when he is in the middle of a murder attempt?

Rome calls my name, but I am not listening. Orlando will get him out of here. Orlando is good like that—thinking of the whole picture, rather than a simple squabble.

I punch the senator a second time, enough to make him lose hold of his fist. I pry the offending ring off his finger like a savage, gritting my teeth when it proves stubborn against sliding over his knobby knuckle.

People are shouting. The governor herself is calling my name to ask for more details of what exactly is going on. The quartet has stopped playing their beautiful music.

None of that matters now. I need to get my blood back if I want to protect the men I brought to this dog and pony show.

Senator Collins cries out, but the second his revolutionary fellows swarm to his aid, I am a woman possessed. The senator cries like the spoiled brat he is, his eyes wide while he swears and spits on the ground. I twist his finger joint until I feel a crack of his finger and know I have broken the bone.

Good.

The ring slides off and I bolt for the exit, following on the tails of Orlando and Rome with the ring in my fist.

This wasn't the night I was hoping to have, but it is surely the night I expected.

20

DOOMED DOUBLE DATE

The flowers and phone calls from the governor have done little to quell the fury in my soul. It's been three days since the governor's party, yet I still find myself wrapped in silent rage that a senator would take my blood in plain sight of an entire party, and no one stopped him but me.

Even as I get out of the car in the parking lot of the movie theater, I slam the door a little too forcefully.

While I want to stomp into the theater because that is the only body language I seem to have today, Rome takes his sweet time getting out of the driver's seat. He makes me wait for him to come around to my side of the car.

"Are you sure you want to see a movie tonight? We can always reschedule," he offers.

"No. My life isn't going to change in the slightest, just

like history. I mean, why should the senator be arrested for attempted murder? Taking my blood is no big deal, right?"

Rome purses his lips but doesn't fuel my fire. To his credit, I've been like this for days, and he has held his tongue. Rome lets me vent and boil over, taking my temper in stride.

He has class, while I have apparently lost all sense of decorum completely.

Rome is without his suit jacket tonight, but his attempt at casual is still fitted black slacks and a white dress shirt with the cuffs rolled. His silver belt buckle is perfectly in place, showing off his trim waist.

He is beautiful while I am a bucket of anger.

He offers me his arm, which I take with a huff. "Three days and no coverage of Senator Collins being held to account. It all happened in a room filled with witnesses, and nothing. I called up the precinct to give my statement, and nothing."

"Did you talk to my father?"

"No. His deputy. Officer Lampert."

I grumble at the misstep. "He's the worst. A complaint to him is useless."

"Clearly." Rome brushes his fingers over mine, which are tucked into the crook of his elbow. "Just say the word and I will handle the senator."

"I don't want you to intervene. Don't you see that? It's always you cleaning up the mess my people are making. I want the actual justice system to perform actual justice. It's their one job, and they turn a blind eye anytime they have to look at protecting a vampire."

Rome chuckles at my temper, which he knows I hate. His neck shrinks. "Sorry. It's the wrong time to tell you how sexy you are when you get all worked up like this, so I won't say it."

I shoot him a wry look as we cross the walkway to the theater. "What stellar self-control you have."

A few people snap pictures of us on our way in, but I pretend not to notice.

Rome is good at keeping his eyes forward, as well, making him the perfect man to date. Anyone else would have been scared off long ago.

I guess we are dating. We didn't have a conversation about it, but we have fallen into a rhythm of being near each other without the veil of distance I insisted upon when he first returned.

I don't know what to make of us, so I ignore the issue completely.

Yes, I am quite the adult.

When we make it into the foyer and buy our tickets, I catch sight of my brother on the other side. I wave him down, only slightly calmed by the sight of my favorite family member. "Hey, Declan, I..." But I stop short when I see Lucas coming out of the bathroom. "Declan, I thought I told you I was bringing Rome. I'm sorry!"

My brother's personal life is his own. Coming out of the closet to people should be his choice, not something that's sprung on him. Rome doesn't know Declan has a boyfriend. I didn't mean to out my brother with no warning like this.

Rome touches the hilt of his gun because that's his default whenever I get spooked. "What's wrong?"

Declan dons a brave smile, rolling his shoulders back. "Nothing's wrong." He shakes Rome's hand, then turns his chin toward me. "I knew Rome was coming. You told me. I figured it wouldn't be so bad if Rome knew. Telling your special guy might pave the way for me one day telling the sheriff."

I marvel up at my brother, proud of him for taking this big step that I know frightens him. Declan is a private person, which I understand. Everything we did was photographed when we were kids, so we fought for each secret to remain our own.

"Declan, that's wonderful." I lean up on my toes and kiss my brother's cheek.

Rome frowns at the both of us. "Tell me what?"

Declan motions for Lucas to join us, since he was hanging back in the periphery until his cue. "Rome, this is my boyfriend, Lucas."

Rome's eyebrows shoot into his hairline, but to his credit, he doesn't embarrass himself. His pitch climbs as he fights to remain relaxed. "Oh! Um, good to meet you,

Lucas. I didn't realize this was a double date. Rome." He cringes when he realizes Declan already introduced him, and he has never needed to tell people who he is.

The three of them do this cute dance of silently feeling each other's reaction out, making sure everyone is okay with each other's presence. Rome is concerned that Declan's boyfriend might not want to double date with a vampire, and Declan is worried that Rome will make a rude comment on the fact that my brother has always been secretly gay.

Lucas and I take the lead, breaking the awkward tension with a hug. "I love the stilettos, sis. You're almost up to my nose with them on."

I snicker and loop my arm through Lucas', leading the way to the concession stand. "Thank you. Only the best for the best. Now, Declan didn't mention if you have a weak stomach. I'm thinking the jumbo popcorn and a hot dog with all the fixings on top. If I'm going to watch a movie with carnage, I need to do it up right."

Lucas chuckles as we order way too much food, placing bets on which of us is going to throw up first.

Rome and Declan chat quietly together while we find our seats. It makes my heart happy to see something so normal happening in plain sight.

We are on a double date, like a normal couple.

Rome takes his seat beside me, pressing a kiss to my

cheek. "You could have given me a heads up. I think my voice went up an entire octave."

I feed him a piece of popcorn. "It wasn't my story to tell. Declan trusts you. That's big. My father and Fintan don't even know he's gay."

Rome beams with pride. "After the movie, let's hang out, the four of us. I like this, doing normal things. Do we like Lucas? Is he good enough for Brother of the Year?"

My gosh, Rome is adorable. I have a hard time remaining in the "just dating" phase instead of tumbling headfirst into the "star-crossed lovers" madness in which we used to be mired.

"Love. We love Lucas. He's a good guy. Good to Declan."

Rome threads his fingers through mine as the lights dim and the previews start. "Could we do more normal things like this? I'm all for making statements and pushing the envelope, but this is better." He motions to the screen. "I'm at the movies with my girlfriend." He cuts his gaze to me to size up my reaction to the label we have not previously discussed. "Is that okay? Is this what you want?"

I swallow hard and then nod. "I wouldn't mind that, so long as we take things slower than we used to. I'm still feeling you out."

Rome holds up his hands to prove his innocence. "Not a problem." Then he motions around the theater. "This is nice."

I study his barely concealed smile before I snort at him. "If you think *Silent Grandma* is going to be nice, you didn't see any of the advertisements. You're going to hate it." I grin at him. "I'm so excited!"

Rome leans over and kisses my lips, mesmerizing me with the allure his tongue always holds when it teases mine.

I'm not sure public kissing qualifies as taking things slow, but I am powerless to resist the taste of Rome's cinnamon lips. I hate that my anger was diluted by my attraction to him. My hurt that he left has been polluted by the sweetness of his commitment to remain by my side ever since he returned.

We never got to kiss in public, yet here I am, sucking on his lower lip under the darkened atmosphere of the movie theater.

I don't expect anyone to interrupt me when I am mid-kiss, but when my name is called, I break away from the sweet moment to glance to Rome's other side.

A man in the theater's uniform with a nametag that reads "Manager" is standing beside our seats, staring down at us with barely controlled revulsion. "Excuse me, Madam Deadblood. Your date will have to come with me."

I sit up straighter, frowning up at the manager. "I'm sorry? What's this about?"

Rome sighs, running his tongue over his top row of

teeth to keep his true thoughts tucked inside. "It's fine. I'm going."

"What? I don't understand."

The manager is pale at taking this stance, yet now that he has opened his mouth, he's going all the way. "We have a strict No Vampires Allowed policy."

I guffaw at him. "I happen to know for a fact that's not true." Orlando followed me into this very theater a couple of months ago. "There is no sign on your entrance that says 'No Vampires Allowed'."

The man in his young thirties holds up his hands. "We have the right to refuse anyone, and you, Mister Valentino, are not allowed in this establishment."

Declan stands, his upper lip curled. "On what basis? Racism?"

The manager is garnering more attention than the previews as the other moviegoers turn their heads toward us. "We are happy to refund the price of your ticket."

I grip the armrests, cementing my butt to my seat. "You're not refunding anything because we're not going anywhere."

Rome's touch is light as his fingers feather over the back of my hand. "It's fine. I'll wait in the car." He stands, jerking my heart around in my chest with how quickly he accepts this injustice.

I snarl up at the manager, finally having a solid place where I can direct my anger. "You're kicking him out because he's with me, not because he's a vampire. It's because he is a vampire who is dating a human."

The manager holds up his hands and repeats himself. "We have the right to refuse anyone."

Lucas stands up, addressing the half-packed theater without hesitation. "Is this who you want to be? You can't control the vampires, so you need to control the Last Deadblood? Who in here has the right to tell anyone else who they can or should love?" When no hands go up, Lucas continues, his knuckles gripping the back of his chair. "Now Madam Deadblood is being kicked out of this very theater because she fell in love without the manager's permission."

The manager turns to the crowd, horrified at the boos and the popcorn that is being aimed his way. "No! Madam Deadblood is of course welcome in our establishment. That's not what's happening!"

I stand, loving Lucas for the spin he is putting on the bigotry.

No one will care if a vampire is asked to leave, but they absolutely will notice if I am kicked out.

I stand with a scowl on my face aimed at the manager. "If Rome goes, I go. Enjoy the press that comes with that."

Rome is nothing but class, while my brother, Lucas and I are prepared to tear this place apart on principle.

Declan stands, straightening his cuffs, staring down the manager until the man squirms.

Lucas is my brother's perfect match in every way. Lucas cups his hands around his mouth so his voice carries to the highest row. "If they will tell the Last Deadblood whom she can love, then they will come for you next! Madam Deadblood is boycotting this theater. All who value her freedom should join us in sitting outside to protest."

Leaving without causing his property severe damage is the last thing on my mind, but Lucas' suggestion of a protest is far more civil than me destroying every screen in this place.

Rome's shoulders lower. I can tell this is wearing on him and he just wants to go home. But when the entire theater stands and shuffles to the exit, giving the longest middle finger salute I have ever witnessed to the manager, he takes my hand and jerks his head toward the exit. "I guess we're doing this."

As to be expected, our "normal" double date turned out not to be so normal after all.

21

PEACEFUL PROTEST

What was supposed to be a fun night of horror and popcorn has turned into a boycott line of nearly a hundred disgruntled moviegoers stretched in front of the theater. Once our movie left, everyone called everyone, with people pulling up to add to our numbers every minute.

Then the news crews came.

Luckily, after the first three interviews, Declan did me a solid and fielded the rest of the questions, making sure everyone had the same story and got the best angle of Rome and me.

The manager turned livid, screaming at us to leave, swearing he would call the sheriff if we didn't get off his property. Boy, did the cameras eat that up.

That was twenty minutes ago, so I'm guessing the sheriff is on his way here now.

That will be a fun conversation. My father will not be pleased to see me causing a stir like this. But honestly, what was I supposed to do? Eat my popcorn while my boyfriend waits in the car for the movie to finish? I'm not playing that game.

I am done waiting for the world to evolve. It's time we gave it another push.

Rome and I stand with our hands clasped. My brother is on my other side, while Lucas hems in Rome, his chest puffed to make sure no one gives my boyfriend any trouble.

I love our little family. The four of us, even though Lucas is new to the group, belong exactly here, holding hands and daring the world to tell us where we are allowed to stand.

While Declan and Lucas are fueled with enough indignation to keep each protestor motivated and orderly, Rome is silent, standing at my side as the motionless beacon of controversy, though he's done and said nothing wrong.

He looks tired, not just from the long day, but from life. His winter coat keeps him warm, I'm sure, but there is a chill to his blue eyes that leaves me feeling cold, despite my own winter coverings.

"I'm sorry," I tell him quietly while a chant of "Movies for All!" starts at the far end of the line. "You finally got a night of fun and it's been ruined with purpose. You never get to relax."

Rome doesn't look at me but stares at the parking lot, the muscles in his neck tensed. "It's about what I should have expected. I never thought I cared that people wouldn't want to see us together. I guess sometimes I surprise myself. I do care. I wanted tonight to be fun. I never get to do this." He jerks his head toward the theater behind us. "Go to a movie just for fun. Sit down for a solid ninety minutes and not have a single person need me for anything." He shrugs. "It's fine."

I ball my toes in my shoes, knowing there is nothing I can say to repair the damage that has been done tonight. Even if the manager miraculously repents of his bigotry, it won't matter.

We can't have a normal double date without it becoming a statement. We can't just *be*; we have to *do*.

I squeeze Rome's hand. "It's not fine, and I'm sorry. You're my boyfriend now. I'm sorry this date is a bust."

I handled this all wrong. We are standing up for Rome's rights, but we didn't check in with him to see if he was actually okay, which it is clear he is not.

I didn't even ask him if he wanted to see a horror movie with me. Maybe he hates gory movies.

"Could we go out to eat tomorrow night?" I suggest, wishing I could feel a connection in our joined hands.

He keeps his gaze fixed on the twilit parking lot. "I have to work. Another night."

There's nothing wrong with his reply, but I feel him

slipping away, writing our relationship off as too much drama. Too much work.

Not worth the effort or the risk.

I open my mouth to tell him we can just go home and leave the protest to go on without us, but he nods toward the entrance of the parking lot. "The sheriff is here. Orlando will bail us out, so don't worry about that. They'll put you in a different cell than me, but they won't hurt you. I'll make sure Orlando bails out Declan and Lucas, too, if they are taken in."

The very real notion that my father is about to arrest us dawns on me.

We have the right to protest. We have the right to free speech.

But those things rarely hold water when the issue is vampire rights.

I raise my chin, angry that I am not allowed to go on a normal date with the man I love. When three squad cars park in front of the theater, my palms begin to sweat.

I am not a fan of being trapped. After being abducted three times, the possibility of being shoved in a cell isn't something I can brush off as if it's all no big deal. My breath begins to syncopate as sweat beads on the nape of my neck.

The sheriff gets out of his squad car and moseys over to us, not rushing or looking the least bit flustered. "What seems to be the problem?" he asks of the manager, who races out of the building toward the cops.

"They're causing a scene in front of my theater! No one's buying tickets. They're going to run me out of business!"

The sheriff takes in the long line of people holding hands, forming a barrier that no one has the gall to cross. It's a statement, going into the theater now. It's a clear line drawn that anyone who enters will be going against the Last Deadblood, and spitting in the face of vampire rights.

They would also be risking Rome's wrath, which is no small threat.

Declan trots over to our father, ushering him to me so he can pretend to listen to what I have to say.

Honestly, I don't want to talk to my father. If he's going to arrest me, I'd rather he just get on with it. Rome is upset. Our date is ruined. All I want is a nap, where I can hide under the covers.

"Quite the party you've thrown here," the sheriff says to me, his thumbs in his belt loops.

"Yup." It's all I care to offer. He doesn't want to know my side of things.

Declan isn't as easily defeated. "Coco and I were going to see a movie, and she wanted to bring Rome. The manager refused him service, pretending that they don't allow vampires, which they do. They just didn't want Rome in the theater because of the thing they're doing."

Declan motions to our joined hands, indicating our relationship, which my father thinks is a show for the press without a lick of substance behind it.

What he would say if he knew it was all real... I shudder to think about it.

Declan stares my father down, believing as always that there is good in even the sheriff. "So we all walked out. We're not going to watch a movie when the Last Deadblood's boyfriend isn't allowed inside."

The sheriff runs his hand over his face. "Coco, I thought you were pretending to date Orlando."

"Rome has better availability," I correct him without further explanation. It's cold and false, but I am not getting into the truth of it all now.

The sheriff watches the defiance in my eyes, studying me carefully. "So this is a peaceful protest. No property was damaged?"

I stare up at him, confused at his questioning. "No. We just left the theater. Now we're standing out here in front of it."

The sheriff nods once, then steps back and grabs a bullhorn from his colleague in blue. His voice doesn't generally need amplification, so everyone winces when his cadence booms across the parking lot. "It looks to me like we've got a peaceful protest going, which is well within the law. So long as no property is damaged, we won't interfere.

In fact," he pauses, handing the bullhorn back to the officer, "I belong on this side with my kids and with Rome."

I gape at my father as he moves back toward us. The sheriff stares with purpose at Rome while cameras click and videos capture every movement. My father hugs Rome and kisses him on the cheek, surprising my boyfriend just as much as he shocks me.

The entire line erupts in cheers, with several people waving for more officers to join our line.

"I'm sorry, Son," the sheriff whispers to Rome. "I let businessowners think they could get away with stuff like this. This is my fault because I looked the other way. I'll fix what I broke."

Officer Lampert watches from outside his squad car. My father's second in command looks horrified at a human showing affection to a vampire. His upper lip curls before he gets back into his car and drives away.

I guess if he can't arrest a vampire, Officer Lampert feels there's nothing for him to do here.

Rome clears his throat, nodding once at acknowledge my father's apology. There is a firmness to his expression that warns us not to make him try to talk, or he might display emotion in public.

I understand the need for composure, but as we stand together, I even I am having a hard time keeping a stern face when all I want to do is fall apart.

22

DECLAN'S BOYFRIEND

The sheriff wedges between Declan and myself, grabbing up both our hands to protest the theater's unjust policy of discriminating against vampires.

"What are you doing?" I ask my father, unsure which way is up at this point.

"I'm standing with my kids. Is that a problem?"

I have no idea who this man is or how to answer him, so Declan chimes in. "Of course not."

The sheriff watches as a few officers remain and join the peaceful protest, while others drive off with a disgruntled huff. "That's disappointing. Fintan and Lampert are friends. Maybe Fintan can talk some sense into my deputy."

I snort. "I hope you heard the leap from logic in what you just said."

"A father can hope, can't he? Fintan is a good boy. He'll come around. I'll bet if he was here, he would join us."

I cast him a wry look. "That's sweet. I wonder if I should tell you that Santa Claus isn't real."

My father keeps his eyes on the line of people holding hands that now stretches from one end of the parking lot to the other. "*I* wonder how long it's going to take before Declan introduces me to his boyfriend."

Declan whips his head up at my father, fear replacing the jovial mood. "What?"

My eyes widen as the worst lie ever comes to the surface. "What are you talking about? Declan? A boyfriend?" My awkward laugh convinces no one.

The sheriff's stoic demeanor melts into pure sadness, as if he cannot believe that the distance he has orchestrated in our family has repercussions. As if not caring about Declan's personal life for his entire life couldn't possibly lead to him being kept in the dark. "Come on, Son. I've known for years. But this is the first time I've actually come close to being able to meet your fella."

Declan is thunderstruck, his mouth agape and all color in his cheeks gone. "I... um... I don't know what to say."

The sheriff turns, fixing his eyes on Lucas without wavering. "Lucas Bronson? No felonies. No arrests. Graduated with honors. You've owned your own roofing company for five years, and all your permits are up to date." The sheriff sticks out his hand, shaking Lucas'. My father evaluates Lucas' stunned demeanor in stride. "I'm Elias, Declan's father. It's good to finally meet you, Son."

Lucas gapes at the sheriff. "Yes, Sir. I'm glad to meet me… I mean you. I'm glad to meet you."

The sheriff turns back to Declan, who has tears welling. They spill down his cheeks when he blinks. "What was that, Dad?"

"That's what should have happened months ago, when you first started dating." The sheriff lowers his chin. "And what should have happened years ago, when I suspected you might be gay. I'm sorry I made you afraid to tell me."

Declan is good at hugging. He's good at forgiveness. There's pretty much nothing my loveable brother isn't good at. All it takes is the sheriff making that bold first move, and my brother falls into our father's arms.

My lower lip quivers at the sight, but I hold my composure as best I can. I know the second the press sniffs out emotion in me, they will zoom in closer to capture the moment. From their distance, they can see a father-son embrace, but hear none of the reason behind it.

My brother came out to our father. The sheriff met Declan's boyfriend and nothing bad happened. In fact, they look closer than they've ever been.

Rome pulls me into his side, but I shirk away. "I can't. I'll fall apart if you're nice to me." It's unkind, but it's not meant to be.

"Understood," Rome replies, because of course he understands the need to be in control in public at all times.

I swear, if these two don't stop hugging, I'm going to lose it.

Emotion squeezes my heart until it's near to bursting. Then finally, the sheriff releases his son. The two of them wipe away their tears, sticking close and holding hands to keep the line intact.

The sheriff angles his chin around Rome and me toward Lucas. "You don't have to pretend for me. Come on over and hold my son's hand. This is going to be a long night if the manager doesn't cave. My boy could use the support."

Lucas marches straight over to Declan and sweeps him in a grand embrace, kissing him gently, his lashes moist. "I'm so proud of you."

A few cameras flash, so like it or not, Declan is out on whatever media channel cataloged the affection.

I am so proud of my brother. Finally, he can be himself without pretending. Without holding back.

Without a fake smile.

Declan laughs through his tears, nodding because none of this feels possible. "I'm sorry. I'm sorry it took me so long. Thanks for waiting."

"For you?" Lucas kisses Declan's nose. "I'd wait forever. You're just that worth it."

That tips it. I turn my head away and breathe hard

through pursed lips, forcing myself to stuff down the swell of emotions I do not want to experience in public.

My father straightens, holding my hand again and giving my fingers a little squeeze. "Senator Collins was arrested this morning for extracting an unregulated weapon of mass destruction."

I gape at his abrupt change of topic. "What?"

After a few beats, his words start to sink in.

The senator who tried to steal my blood was arrested? He is being held to account for his actions?

That's a twist I didn't see coming.

My father keeps his eyes on the reporters who are having their best day of work ever. "Sorry it took so long. Getting your blood registered as a weapon worth prosecuting for was more paperwork than I realized."

I fight the urge to back away. "I don't understand what you're doing."

My father's eyes rest on my confusion, repentance plain on his face. "I'm doing what I should have done years ago. Nothing more, nothing less."

Declan grins at the both of us because he loves it when we all get along. "Family dinner Friday night?"

The sheriff nods. "Looking forward to it, so long as you bring your boyfriend. He's one of us now."

Lucas grins through his tears, holding tight to Declan's other hand. "Wouldn't miss it for the world."

The sheriff's chest barrels. "Smile for the cameras, kids.

They've never seen common sense before. If we make it look appealing, maybe they'll join us one day."

Did my father just make a joke?

I have no idea how a simple trip to the movies turned into a protest that changed my father into a normal dad, but as the reporters swarm and the night falls, I realize that maybe I am not alone in my fight to make this city stronger.

Maybe I had help all along.

23

LEAVE ALL OVER AGAIN

After the protest, I drive Rome to my house in silence. Depression is radiating off his shoulders, thickening the air with unsaid condemnations.

After shivering through our protest in the freezing evening air, the manager finally caved. He agreed on camera that all vampires are welcome in the movie theater, and that was that. Everyone celebrated the small victory, thinking it some big step forward.

It was a two-hour-long protest, all so a vampire could sit in a movie theater.

When I pull into my driveway and park, Rome stops me before I exit. "I'm going to sleep at my place tonight," he announces, as if I didn't expect as much.

I nod, knowing he has had a long night filled with disappointment and drama. He wanted no part of any of it. He wanted to take me to a movie and eat red vines.

"I understand," I tell him, my voice hollow. But as I make to open my door, worry sneaks up in my throat, tightening my tone. "Are you taking off again? Are you done with us? I'd rather know now."

Rome turns his chin to me, studying my exposed nerve for the internal damage it is. He purses his lips and then lowers his shoulders, casting aside his cool demeanor. "No. Hey, no. I'm not leaving you. I'm not leaving us. I just know I'm not going to be very good company tonight. I don't want you to have to suffer through my bad mood."

I nod slowly, leaning back in my seat. "What would you do if you went home? How do you christen a bad night?"

Rome reaches across the console so he can play with my fingers. "Lots of stomping around the house like a big, scary man." He shoots me a covert glance. "I might drink too much."

"I've never seen you drink anything more than a glass of wine."

"That's because I save my bad moods for when you're not around. When I'm down like this, I drink my weight in scotch and pass out on the couch. Then I wake up with a hangover and a crick in my neck that I blame on whomever made me drink too much the night before. That way I have two reasons to be mad at them."

"That's logical."

Rome snorts, playing with my fingers. "I get drunk enough to talk to a portrait of my dad, asking him what he would have done—what I should have done. It's not pretty."

"Pity. I only love you when you're pretty."

Rome kisses my fingertips one at a time. "I'm going to be busy the next few days."

"You're leaving," I say again, unable to hide my fear.

I attached myself to a mirage, and not a man.

"No, tré-sur." Rome leans his head against the headrest, turning in his seat to scrutinize my worry. "I did this to you. I made you nervous I would take off over the smallest thing. Over a date that doesn't turn out perfect. I'm sorry, little cannoli." He motions to the house. "You convinced me. I'll come inside. But I really do have to catch up on work this week, so I'll be a bit of a ghost for the next few days. That has nothing to do with you, only the fact that I'm not all that great at delegating."

Rome is still lacking pep in his step, but he isn't as distant now as we walk hand-in-hand to my house.

After a night like tonight, I know he needs a little tenderness. He needs someone to listen to him if he feels like talking, and if he doesn't, I need to respect that. He was the rallying point for a rebellion that, thankfully, turned out well. But all he wanted out of tonight was a little flirting and a movie, and the world deprived him of even that.

Orlando is in the West End tonight, so we have the house to ourselves. I wish we were in a makeout sort of headspace, but neither our damaged relationship nor the events of the evening call for something so lavish.

So I go with simplicity.

Rome doesn't put up a fuss when I make him a cup of chamomile tea while he checks the grounds for any sign of foul play. I bought this land because I wanted plenty of space to keep myself from being stalked, but it seems no matter how careful we are, that worry might always have a valid spot in my mind.

Rome comes back inside after the tea is steeping in his China cup. It's a little civility that I hope to instill into the night, reminding us that we are deserving of beautiful things and peaceful moments.

"Thank you," he says quietly, his hand brushing over my stomach as he kisses my temple. "Maybe tea is a better choice than a bottle of scotch."

"Here's hoping."

When he sits, I move to the refrigerator and pull out the flask of Orlando's blood that Declan drained from him earlier this week, in case Orlando had to be away from me when I needed a dose of the medicine only my big sweetie pie can give. I tip a few drops into my tea and mix it around, pretending it's honey and completely normal.

Rome has a defeated look about him, even as I sit to join him at the counter on the stool beside his. "Things have spun completely out of control. You're mated with my cousin. We're together, but we have to be extra careful because I messed things up between us." He pinches the bridge of his nose. "How is this going to work? I'm in love with you, but you're linked to my cousin? I see the way you two trust each other. You lean on him the way you used to lean on me."

I don't say anything in response. I sip my tea in silence. I want to ask him whose fault that is, breaking the trust between us, but I hardly think pointing out the obvious is helpful.

Rome drinks his tea, but it does nothing to calm him. "We can't have a date night without it turning into a big political statement. I don't have the energy to fight two losing battles. The West End takes up a fair amount of my time. Fighting for us is a whole separate headache."

My lips purse even as relief floods my veins at having the medicine my body craves. "You don't have to endure any headaches you don't want to." I keep my voice level, knowing that if this where Rome ends things, my only course of action is to accept that dating the Last Dead-blood takes patience and thick skin.

I thought Rome had both of those things in his arsenal, but perhaps not.

I don't know how my father did it. I never think of his plight whenever I look back on my parents' marriage. The scrutiny of being the man on my mother's arm meant everything must be perfectly in order. The world is watching, especially with all the moving and shaking my mother did in the political world to move society toward acceptance and civility.

I motion in the direction of the front door, knowing that if Rome wants out, there is nothing I can do to stop him. "There's the door. You know how to make good use of it."

Rome keeps his eyes on his tea. "If it was just you and just me, I would marry you tonight, if marriage was legal for me. But it's never going to be just us. It's the whole world weighing in on every move we make. We can't watch a movie without a protest breaking out." He shakes his head at the state of the world. "That's not a relationship. I know myself, Coletta. This is not something I can maintain." He sets down his cup and scratches a spot on his elbow. "But the other option is to be without you, and I can't stomach that again. I tried and it didn't take. I want to be with you; I only wish I could erase all the other factors."

I purse my lips, fighting to keep any aggression or resentment out of my tone. "Well, the good news is that you can walk away. You have options. You can go back to the West End and find someone new." I motion to my form. "I don't have those options. I will always be the Last Deadblood. I can't change that." My voice falls to a whisper, knowing I am about to break the last point that tethers us together. "I deserve to be with a man who wants all of me. Not someone who loves part of me and tolerates the rest."

Rome nods. "Well put."

I clear my throat, pretending that I am not devastated, and that this breakup is a mere hiccup I will forget about in a few months. "Very well. Enough people have seen us in public that we don't have to keep up appearances. If you can pretend we're together, I think that would be enough. We don't have to be near each other all that often to keep the charade going."

Rome looks at me with surprise rounding his eyes. "You're okay with me leaving?"

"I have no intention of begging a man to stay. If you want to be with me, here I am. If who I am is too much work, then go."

Rome's nose scrunches. "You say it like I'm calling you high maintenance. That's not what this is. I don't want to have to make a big political statement just to take you on a date."

I shrug, my voice hollow. "Then you can't have what you want if you stay with me. This is my life. When I lost my first tooth, the papers covered it. Every time Fintan set me up on a blind date, the guy got a full spread done on him in case he turned out to be the man who ended up with the Last Deadblood." I lean back in my seat with a sigh. "What you're forgetting is that *I* didn't get to see the movie, either. One day, you'll date someone else, and you'll get to sit through the whole thing, eat all the popcorn and enjoy your time out. I will never get that chance if I have a date with me. That's why Declan and I do so much together. People leave me alone for the most part if I'm just with family." I keep my eyes on my teacup. "I stood up for you tonight because you deserve better. If this is my lot in life, then I'm going to use it for my platform's advantage because I am not a victim. I am not simply a means to an end. If they want to point their cameras at me, they're going to listen to what I have to say."

Rome lowers his head. "I'm scum. I didn't even think about how tonight affected you. You picked the movie, too. You're the one who actually wanted to see that crapfest, and you didn't get the chance." He closes his eyes as self-loathing washes over him. "Your brother got outed, and I'm sitting here feeling sorry for myself. Your family stood up for me, yet it's too exhausting for me to be cared about?" He shakes his head at himself. "I told you I wouldn't be good company tonight."

I drain my tea and move to the sink so I can be done with this conversation that seems to be going in a circle. "That's just as well. I'm going to bed anyway. Figure out where it's all going to land for you and leave me a post-it note when you decide."

Rome stands, beelining to my side. His eyes burn into the side of my face, seeming to see right through my cool charade to my aching heart. "What do you want, Coletta? If you could have what you wanted, tell me what it is.

There are too many voices weighing in on us. I want to hear from you."

I let out a joyless one-noted laugh through my nose. "I can't have what I want, so I make the best with the space I have."

Rome takes a chance with his life and rests his palm on the small of my back. "Coletta. Please. I need to know you. Tell me where you are so we can find each other."

I turn my chin and blink up at him, frustrated with myself when emotion puts pressure behind my eyes. "I would want to run away. Far, far away with the man who wants to be with me. I would want to hide so I can hear my own voice again. I would want to make the most of the years I have left, and leave the world to burn however it pleases." My voice catches on the last note, so I stop talking.

Rome turns my body and cups my face with such tenderness, it's like he is afraid I might be made of glass.

If only. How I wish I was fragile, or that it mattered that I might be breakable. As it is, I must be hardened steel at all times.

His lips descend on mine, taking their time because we are both shaken.

Taking things slow was a good idea, because at the first taste of his mouth, all I want is to drown myself in the sea of his affections. His lips are soft and careful, yet still not hesitating to take what they want and remind me of what I need.

"Run away with me," Rome breathes between kisses. "Coletta, please."

My heart spasms in my chest. "What? Rome, we can't."

"We can. I can leave the West End to its devices," he pleads and then kisses me again. His body is pressed to mine, making good use of our time alone. "And you can leave behind the rest of the world that tells us we don't belong together."

The offer is tempting, but only makes me more depressed. I want what Rome is suggesting, but it's not real. It's a mirage of a life we can never have. We care about the plight of the vampire people too much to walk out when they need us most.

"If I love you, I have to stay here," I counter. "I have to fight for your family, for your people. I can't be selfish with you."

Yes, I can. I want to. But I know that's not love.

Rome's forehead marries itself to mine, his cinnamon breath fanning across my nose so all I feel, all I smell, all I am is him. "Think more on it. I'm breaking, Coletta. I feel it in my bones." He leans heavily on the edge of the counter because the weight of this conversation is too much.

I understand completely.

Rome brushes his nose across mine. "I need to be away

from all of this, and I want to be there with you. Only you. Only us."

Tears prick my eyes as his plea and pledge hit parts of my soul I didn't realize I had left scattered about for his perusal.

We can't go away just the two of us. I am linked to Orlando. At the very least, it would be the three of us.

But I don't say any of that. I sink further into the sin of our kiss, letting myself believe that a quiet life might be possible, and that there might be a reality for the two of us to leave the world behind so we can breathe and rest together, because that is how we design it.

I need to tell him no. Obviously we can't run away from Mayfield. The West End would fall apart without him. I am running a business. I can't just up and disappear.

Though, I can run things remotely. That's not a problem.

I can take my foot off the gas a little and let myself coast towards a bliss I never thought I would have.

I let Rome's arms cocoon me in this dare of a thought as it tempts me with its possibility.

Could I really do this?

"I need time," I whisper as his lips trail along my jaw. "I don't know the right answer. I don't want to say no, but I can't say yes. I need to think."

Rome nods, his cheek moving against mine, intoxicating me further with his cologne and is presence. "I can wait. Just the fact that you would consider running away with me is enough to calm me down for now. Thank you."

"I love you," I admit, though he doesn't deserve to hear something pure like that. "I'm all turned around."

Rome nods. "Me, too. But if we love each other, we can figure this out. I can give you time, tré-sur."

I kiss his lips, confused and left with a storm cloud of confusion that creates a haze I cannot dismiss.

I want to be with him. But I don't know how to ignore the world that has never once let me make my own choices.

Rome's lips lull me with their sweetness. For the moment, I pretend I am a woman with a bright future, and that I can be with the man I want.

It's a beautiful thought, and one I hope doesn't leave me in the morning.

24

AWKWARD FAMILY DINNER

It's been three days since Rome asked me to run away with him, and I am no closer to being able to answer that crazy request. I was certain he would have left by the time the sun rose, but in the middle of the night, Rome let himself into my bedroom, tiredly asking if he could sleep beside me.

The conversation shook us both, so we have been on the edge of giving each other space and occasionally clinging too tight to fend off the worry that often creeps up. Turns out, our lives are too chaotic to go through alone.

I wanted to call my brother and make a lame excuse to get me out of family dinner tonight, but this is Lucas' first taste of being in the Kennedy home during a family night. Declan would be mad at me if I bailed when he needs me to be his backup.

Still, I wait in my car until Declan pulls up. No way am

I going into the house with only Father and Fintan in there. I need my backup, too.

When Declan and Lucas emerge from his car, they both have a winded look to them, as if they had to psych themselves up to come here, too. Declan slaps his hands together and rubs with unconvincingly manufactured excitement. "Glad you didn't back out of coming. Ready for some food we didn't have to cook?"

I shake my head. "Not really. I'm here for you, you realize. I don't have the energy for this, but I'm here for you."

Declan bumps my fist with his. "I know, and I appreciate it."

Lucas kisses my cheek and then wraps an arm around Declan and an arm around my shoulders, corralling us to the porch. "It's going to be great. You'll see. Now the both of you need to stop looking like someone forced you here at gunpoint. We can do this. Family fun. Yay!"

I snicker at Lucas' show of enthusiasm. I haven't smiled all day, so the motion is a foreign relief. "Remember that optimism. So sweet. So naïve. It won't last long."

One day, I might be the kind of daughter who brings a casserole to family dinners, but for now, it's all I can do to force myself to show up. "Hey, Sheriff," I greet my father when he opens the door to my childhood home.

My father is wearing a smile and a red apron. "Right on time. Good to see you, Coco. I hope you like crab, because I boiled them myself. First time for everything, right?"

Well, I'm allergic to crab, but whatever. I'm not hungry anyway.

Declan grimaces. "Actually, Dad, Colette's..."

My brother stops talking when I reach around Lucas to pinch him to shut him up. If my father doesn't know the basics of my makeup, then I don't feel the need to educate him now.

There's a nervousness to my father's smile, like he's hoping I don't take one look at him and bolt.

His fears are not completely unfounded, being that I nearly didn't come at all tonight.

I put my father out of his misery and step onto the stained beige carpet that should have been replaced years ago.

"Smells good in here," I offer.

Fintan stands, his attempt at a smile falling woefully short as he greets his brother. "Declan. Good to see you. Dad told me about your... you know, your situation." He motions to Declan and Lucas awkwardly. It's as if Fintan assumes saying the word "gay" aloud might cause him to suddenly develop a taste for dudes.

My gosh.

Lucas is ever the perfect fit to any circumstance, even one as uncomfortable as this. He stretches out his hand to Fintan, shaking it without a hint of ire. "Nice to meet you. I'm Lucas."

Fintan nods, his body language still stiff. He grunts,

which I think is supposed to mean "Nice to meet you. I've never shaken the hand of a gay man before."

I roll my eyes at what is about as good a reaction as Fintan is capable of giving in this situation.

The sheriff calls us to the table, no doubt sensing that we need things like food to distract us and make us appear normal. "Crab boil, salad, and strawberries. Don't everyone jump at the pot at once. Your old man learned a new trick this week. I've been watching the cooking channel, and I think it's paying off. After the protest, I thought we could use something special."

I didn't realize my father watched anything but the news. To imagine him with anything other than a gruff personality is akin to an image of him suddenly doing a pirouette and dancing around the living room.

We sit down to eat while I play the part of the stereotypical waif, picking at my salad and fruit. It's the best I can do. If I eat crab, I will break out in hives and ruin the evening.

We make it through the dinner without incident, mostly because Fintan is mute with discomfort, and therefore can't be a problem. Though, as we clear the table to set up for poker and dessert, Fintan takes a shot at me. "I can't believe you didn't bring your fake boyfriend to family dinner. Can't you just picture Rome at the table, sipping on a blood bag while we eat?"

I keep my eyes on the dishes while I rinse my plate in

the sink. I wish I was strong enough not to take the bait. "You know very well your former best friend eats food just like we do."

Fintan blanches, then uses two fingers to mime fangs coming down from his gums. "Can you imagine if you had to actually kiss him? Luckily the world believes your little scandal if you just hold his hand."

"Uh-huh. Declan, give me a hand with these dishes?" I don't want to steal him from Lucas' side, but if Declan doesn't step in and diffuse my temper, Fintan is going to be wearing his dessert home, which I'm guessing isn't how families usually end their meals together.

Declan trots over to me. "Fintan, grab the serving bowls and bring them to the sink. I'll bag up some left-overs for you. But I call the last crab leg." He rubs his stomach. "So good."

Fintan meanders away from me, effectively saving his life from my wrath.

Declan pats my back while I exhale.

"Remind me why I'm here?" I ask him forlornly.

"You're here because you love me, and you know I will never forgive you if you leave Lucas and me alone with Dad and Fintan."

"Right. The reason that means you owe me a meal that won't make me break out in hives."

"Deal." The two of us wash and dry the dishes while

Fintan and Father set up poker at the dining room table. Lucas portions out the dessert.

If only we could just call it a night.

A little voice in my head tempts me with a mischievous, *"If you ran away with Rome, you wouldn't have to worry about any of this. You could leave the sheriff behind. Fintan's snide, controlling comments would be a distant memory."*

I purse my lips as I move to my spot at the dining room table, taking up my cards that father deals us with his brows furrowed. Lucas and Declan are talking quietly, smiling because this is such a normal night, and they get to enjoy it together.

My father tugs at his collar, shifting in his seat uneasily. All night, his smile has been forced, but I chalked that up to him being unpracticed in the artform of happiness or hosting. But now that I look closer, I see he's got something on his mind.

Perhaps a whole lot of somethings.

"Everything okay, Sheriff?" I ask him quietly.

He straightens and arranges his cards in his hand. "I've got all my kids here, plus another kid I get to keep around. What could possibly be wrong on a night like this?"

"You tell me," I want to say, but I keep my mouth shut. I did my due diligence. If the sheriff wants to speak up, that was his window.

His gaze cuts to me. "Anything you want to tell me?"

My eyes widen because I know the answer to that without having to pause to think it through. "No."

No and never. You stay out of my life, and I stay out of yours. That's the only way we work.

But before the first hand is played, the sheriff sets down his cards and presses his hands together, leaning his elbows on the table. "Boys, it's time. Things are getting worse, and Colette should know."

Declan pales, whipping his head toward our father and then gaping with horror at me. "What?"

Fintan gets that authoritative older brother look about him. "Dad, I don't think that's a good idea. We've got it handled."

The sheriff squeezes his fist atop the table, staring at his hand as if it is his source of strength. "Enough secrets. If I want my kids to be honest with me, I have to set the trend." He waves toward the kitchen. "I've been gearing up for this talk all week. It's time for me to come clean. Did you think I made crab boil for the fun of it?"

Lucas and I lock eyes, suddenly aware that there has been much going on beneath the surface that neither of us were aware of.

This is going to be a long night.

25

THE SHERIFF'S SECRET

Ice replaces any warmth in my veins when my brothers tilt their chins downward, refusing to meet my eyes.

I am completely confused. We were having a normal night with a lavish dinner my father made by himself. Was all of that a prop for him getting me here? Is he about to drop some unforeseen bomb on my head?

I look to Declan, who is doing his best to appear invisible in plain sight. "What did I miss? Declan?"

Lucas stands. "This seems like a family matter. I'll wait in the car and give you all some privacy."

The sheriff shakes his head and points to Lucas' chair. "Have a seat, Son. You should know because things are getting worse. Declan will need the support if everything keeps going how it is."

Neither of my brothers will look at me or open their

mouths to speak, so I turn my chin, casting my inquisitive gaze across the table to my father. He has his eyes closed as if sitting in prayer, begging God for better times. "There's no easy way to say this, so let's just get it over with."

The long pause tests the bounds of my self-control, especially when Declan gets up from the table to leave.

"Sit down, Declan," the sheriff instructs. "There have been developments."

My throat is dry, but I manage to get my point across. "Will someone please tell me what's going on? Why is there something you all know about that I don't? Did I miss something?"

This is it. The sheriff is going to tell me the war is back on. Some vampire did something stupid, and we're going to overreact in a massive retaliation, as is our way. My stomach churns at the prospect.

I won't do it. If they need my blood for weaponization, I won't give it to them.

The sheriff doesn't address my fretting or my temper, which swings as wild as his when provoked. "A while ago I went to the doctor. He found a lump."

My thoughts come to a screeching halt.

What?

In all the chaos of our city life, something as grim as a lump doesn't make sense.

My flabbergast cannot be measured. I grip the edge of

the table, willing my words to stay in place so they don't fling out of me unchecked.

My father found a lump.

"I had a surgery last year to remove it, but it's back." This must be the part the boys didn't know about, because they both stiffen.

I hold up my hand. "Wait, a year ago? You had surgery a year ago on a lump and you're just now telling me?" I glare my hurt at Declan. "You knew?"

Declan keeps his head lowered. "Dad didn't want us to tell you. His body, his call."

Lucas looks like he wants to melt into the floor to get away from this conversation.

Welcome to the family, Lucas.

My throat is dry, my palms dampening with sweat. "Why?" Then I laugh hysterically, forcing Fintan to startle at my unbalanced volume. "Why tell me now? Why not keep on pushing me out of the family?"

The sheriff presses his hands to the tabletop. "I'm telling you now because it's back. The lump is back and it's inoperable. It's on a lymph node this time, which apparently is the worst place to have one. Doctor gave me a few months if I do chemo and go through all the crap of it. A few weeks if I don't."

Fintan leans forward, floored at this new information. Of course, he goes into control-mode. "You're obviously doing chemo. We're not taking this thing without a fight."

The sheriff sighs, closing his eyes again. In that simple movement, I can see how truly tired he is. He doesn't have it in him to fight, to deteriorate with gusto. He wants to decide how sick he will let us see him.

I know this because I am my father's daughter.

My brothers argue with great passion, begging and ordering him to go through the treatment if it will prolong his life.

I say nothing because I am in complete and total shock.

My father is dying. He's sitting across from me, and this cancerous lump is eating him from the inside out.

My father is dying.

My father is dying.

My father is dying.

No matter how many times I say it to myself, the horror doesn't fade.

I don't realize I am standing until my feet are taking me out the front door and down the street to my car.

When my fingers touch on the handle, Declan's shout stills my exit. "Colette, wait!"

I blink across the stretch of grass at him, unsure if I am about to cry, or if I have hit a new level of heartbreak that tears cannot touch.

When Declan wraps me in his arms, I shove him away with a ferocity I didn't realize I possessed. "You knew!" I shout at him, taking out my anger on the only member of my family who loves me. "How long did you all know, and you didn't say a thing to me?"

Declan hangs his head and shoves his hands in his pockets. "Dad was diagnosed two years ago. He didn't want us to tell you."

My finger jabs in his direction with all the venom in my soul. "You know that was the wrong call! I am part of this family. Gosh, how many times do I have to try to convince you all of that? Just because the sheriff sent me away to get rid of me for all those years doesn't make me any less a part of it all."

Declan's head shoots up. "Come on. You know that's not why you were sent away. It was too dangerous here. You were abducted three times! Even if the doctor who did wonders on you lived in Mayfield, we still would have had to send you away. It wasn't safe!"

The truth of his words smacks me with fresh psychosis. It took me a long time to be able to walk to my car at night without having a panic attack.

After my last abduction, it took me a long time to be able to walk without assistance.

I point to the pavement, taking my stand once and for all. "I am not a second-class citizen in this family! I'm out. I mean it. My life is my business if the sheriff's cancer was his."

Declan raises his hands in surrender. "Your life has always been your business. You keep the sheriff out just as much as he keeps himself from you. You're the same person, Coco. Two bulls stuck in the same arena until the end of time."

I gasp at his assessment, scandalized that he would jump to such a reckless conclusion.

Anger boils and mutates, turning to resentment until melancholy sets in when I realize I don't want to look at a single member of my family right now.

"I have nothing to say to you. You're my best friend, yet you kept something like this from me?"

Declan lowers his chin in surrender. "It was the wrong call. Believe me, I wanted to tell you. I've had no one to talk to about it all. As angry as you are right now, I've been going through this alone, taking Dad to doctor's appointments and watching him accept that this is the way things are going to play out. I'm losing my father, too, Coco. No one is going to handle this well. If I did it wrong, then frankly, I'm surprised that's the only time I've made a mistake. These past two years have been Hell."

I want to punish Declan for this, but he looks so defeated that I don't have it in me to push him further over the edge.

Lost. All I feel is lost. I don't know how to deal with this sense of utter overwhelm.

So I go with my gut, which usually tells me to run.

Blame it on my upbringing, being sent away when things grew too intense. Blame it on me being a giant chicken who can only handle so much. Whatever led me to this flaw in my personality, part of me knows it might never go away.

For the moment, I decide to go with it. "Goodnight, Declan."

"I'm sorry! Please, Coco-bean. Stay and let's figure this out. You're doing that thing where you run instead of fight. We need to fight about this. Please! I am worth the fight!"

My hand freezes on the handle of my car door. "You are, but this isn't." I point to the house I grew up in, unable to say another word about it.

Whatever my brother wants to say to me, I don't hear it. I'm not sure I can hear anything that might resemble reason right now.

I am gone, and I have no interest in ever coming back.

26

NOT ALRIGHT

My aching heart guides the way as I step into my car and drive off, unsure where I am heading or if I'll know where I am when I get there.

My eyes fog over as emotion chokes me, making oxygen difficult to come by.

My father is dying. My father won't live to see another Christmas.

Everything hurts. My bones are heavy while being simultaneously hollow. My father is dying...

...and nobody thought it important to tell me.

I pass by the road that would take me to my house, unsure where I am going, other than a nebulous "away."

Yes, that sounds like the perfect place to go. Away from here. Away from all of this.

I call Rachel, doing my best to sound nonchalant, though my voice rings tinny and falsely sweet. "Rachel, I'm going out of town for a few..." I'm not sure how long I will be gone. "I'll be away for a while. Do you still have the numbers of the other branch managers, should you run into trouble?"

I can practically hear Rachel's eyes rattling in her head with a vigorous nod. "Of course. Don't worry about a thing. I've been hoping you would trust me enough with the salon to really step away. I won't let you down."

When I end the call, it's my hope that my nerves will have settled and the desire to run will have quelled.

When my palms begin to sweat all over again, I know I can't go home, not even to grab a change of clothes. I know if I go back there, Declan will be at my house, waiting to talk things out.

I'm not ready to talk.

It's a thing of luck that my phone rings before I end up in another state without thinking anything through. "Rome?" I see that I've missed a call from him.

"You sound off. You alright, little cannoli?"

No. Nothing will ever be alright again. But instead of the truth, I parse it with a hesitant "I'm not sure."

"Declan called me. Said he screwed up and you were upset. What's going on?"

I curse aloud, my eyes tearing up as emotion begins to catch up with me. Apparently, I can't outrun my regrets, though I can sure as heck try.

"Talk to me, Coletta," Rome prods.

"No. I don't want to talk about any of it."

"Then I'll sit with you, and we can be silent together. Tell me where you are. I can come to you."

Damn him for saying the exact right thing.

My lower lip quivers. My vision blurs, so I pull over, knowing that even though I don't have the shakes and my body isn't betraying me, I need to take a minute before I lose sight of the road altogether. "I don't know where I'm going. I had a rough night with my family, so I left. I'm driving until... until it doesn't feel like this."

"Keep talking to me, Coletta. I'm here."

I am certain no one will ever get me like this man does without even trying.

My voice catches as tears fall without hesitation. "I need to get out of here."

Suddenly the world stops spinning and everything stills. My worry that I won't accomplish enough in my time left deserts me and is replaced by an eerie silence that pushes all clutter and chaos to the periphery, where I cannot see or hear it.

I don't need to think about anything. I don't need to feel.

I need to run.

And I know just who will run away with me.

Rome's promise rings through my body. "I can take you wherever you want to go, tré-sur. Just say the word, and we're gone."

"Yes," I choke into the phone. "You asked me to run away with you. I'm saying yes. Right now. Let's go."

Rome pauses, and then spills his soul with an intensity that clenches around my heart. "You mean it?"

"Yes. Please, Rome. Let's run away together."

Relief is palpable in his breathy reply. "I'm heading home right now to pack a bag. How long are we running away for?"

I don't have that answer, so I give it my best guess. "I don't want to come back. Let them all burn, Rome. Take me away from here. I can't do this anymore." Worry creases my brow. "And I can't go home. Can you stop by my place and pack a bag?"

"Already texting Orlando to do that. He'll send us with the flask of his blood, too. It's done. It's taken care of." He exhales with relief I wish I could feel. "Thank you, tré-sur. I need this. I need to be gone, and I need to be gone with you."

"I'll meet you at the salon. We'll take my car. Hurry, Rome. I don't know where we're going, but I need to be there right now. I can't stay in Mayfield a second longer." The itch has started in my soul. The longer I sit here in this city where my father is dying, the worse the itch gets. "Get me out of here," I whisper, desperate for relief from this pain I cannot quantify.

"I know where we can go. Only Orlando knows about it, so it's secure and far enough away from the city. Life can be better, Coletta. I promise. I will give us a better life than this."

"I love you, Rome. I should have left with you days ago when you said you wanted to take off. You've been sitting with this sandpaper in your soul for this long? I can't take another hour of this. I love you. I only want to be with you."

"Mm." I crave the low throaty noise he makes. It's equal parts satisfaction and unquenched desire. "I'll drive us somewhere that we can be alone." I can hear him opening drawers. I imagine him hurriedly packing.

"Thank you. Thank you for understanding how badly I need this."

"I know you," Rome reminds me, which, as it turns out, is the perfect thing to say.

I hang up because if Rome says one more sweet thing to me, I will tear his clothes off the second I see him, which I know isn't the right thing to do when I am out of sorts.

I drive to the salon once my tears clear enough for me to safely navigate behind the wheel.

For the next chunk of time after I park in the back lot of the salon, I let out the brunt of my ugly tears, sobbing by myself because I don't want Rome to see me so uncontrolled.

I had such high hopes for this place—so many dreams of a better life, a better city, a better way for us all.

Maybe Mayfield doesn't deserve a gift like optimism. I

tried my best, and I failed. The salon will keep going, but I'm out.

I don't even realize how much time has passed when knuckles rap on my window. Orlando's back is to me, even as I roll down my window, sucking back snot and tears. "Here," he says, shoving a handkerchief through the window at me. It's clear he hates the sight of emotion so much that he keeps his back to me.

"Th-Thanks, Orlando." I dab at my eyes and then examine the dainty white square.

There are two initials embroidered on the edge, and they take me a minute to decipher.

CK?

My heart stammers in my chest when I realize this is the handkerchief I'd wished for weeks ago when my heart was broken. I'd imagined my mother dabbing my worries away with her handkerchief. I don't even know if she owned one in real life. But in my imagination, she would wipe my tears with a white cloth that had her initials embroidered on the edge.

Chondra Kennedy.

It is the perfect gift to see me through to this next phase in my life.

Orlando clears his throat. "Give me a name."

"Huh?"

"Who upset you?"

I shake my head. "No one who needs to be fitted with cement shoes. Just family stuff getting out of hand."

A long pause hangs in the night air between us while I hiccup through my tears.

Orlando shoves his hands in his pockets. "You know I'll take care of things for you, right? If there's a problem, you talk to me about it, and I'll make it go away."

I chuckle through my sadness, grateful that I am one of the few people who understands that this is an oath of loyalty not many will receive from someone in the Valentino family.

"I love you, too, Orlando."

"Rome's making a few calls in the car. There's a flask of my blood in the cooler in the trunk. A few drops every night, and you'll be just fine. I know where he's taking you, so I'll come by every week to make sure the flask stays full. Your medication is packed, too, so don't forget to take it."

I hiccup at his back, since he still won't look at my puffy features. "You're not going to try to convince me to stay?"

Orlando knows not to look directly at me. Maybe he's keeping his eyes averted because emotion makes him uncomfortable, or maybe he is preserving my pride because he understands I am just as private a person as he has always been. "No. You've given your pound of flesh to Mayfield. Get out while you're still standing. I'll handle things from here."

It's a lofty promise, but I don't argue that he will need more help than he has.

He reaches in through the window but doesn't turn around. He grabs onto my fingers, connecting us because we have been through too much to pretend goodbyes don't affect us.

"Goodbye, Orlando my love," I whisper, saying the words that once made us chuckle. But I do love him, jaded and cold as I often am.

"Goodbye, Colette my dove," he replies without hesitation.

When Orlando releases my fingers, I roll my window back up and blow my nose into the handkerchief. It's all a jumbled mess, a storm in my chest that might never go away.

When Rome gets out of his car and stands outside my window, the tears start all over again. Orlando and Rome converse quietly with Orlando giving him what looks like a stern warning.

I get it. I'm bad for business. I'm bad for the family. I should marry a man my father picks out because I should trust him with my future, even though he won't trust me with his present predicaments.

My chest aches when my door opens, and Rome extends his hand to help me out. I expect him to lead me to his car, but instead he tugs me into his arms, holding me firm to his chest. "Let's get you out of here," he whispers in my ear.

Both my arms wrap around his neck. "I'm sorry," I whimper. "I'm falling apart all over the place. I shouldn't have involved you in my family's drama. But I can't stay here anymore."

Rome holds me tighter, a current of anger stiffening his tone. "You don't get to apologize for needing me. That's not how this works. You've got a lot on your shoulders. If something proves to be too much, you'd better not hesitate to call me." He tilts my chin up so he can kiss my lips with a bruising pressure. "Promise me. Your problems are mine, understood?"

I shake my head, unused to anyone speaking to me like this. "Only if yours are mine, too."

Rome's angular jaw firms. I can tell he would very much like to argue, but I've made too solid a point. "Very well. Looks like we've got a lot of talking to do during our little trip away." He kisses me again, settling a handful of the fearful parts inside of me that I assumed would never calm down. "Let's get you into the car. I'm driving."

Rome doesn't part from me until he has guided me into the passenger's seat of my car, even going so far as to help me with my seatbelt.

Orlando loads up the trunk for us. "Don't stop until you get there, okay?" he warns Rome. "No one can see you've got her with you, or they will assume you stole her.

You know how people get about the Last Deadblood. Now that she's such a political figure, they're not going to take her absence lying down. Park in the garage and keep all the shades drawn."

I can tell Rome wants to give him a tart "no kidding" sort of response, but my boyfriend takes the edicts in stride, knowing the more Orlando tries to protect him, the more Orlando is showing he loves us.

Then Orlando leans his head into the car, his eyes filled with purpose. Neither of us says a word. We lean in like magnets about to be separated for far too long, and press a kiss to the side of each other's mouths.

Rome starts up the car and drives carefully out onto the main road, but not before I catch sight of Declan's car turning down the street, no doubt driving to the salon to look for me.

Your concern for me is too little too late, brother.

"You want me to turn around so you can go talk to Declan?" Rome asks, his eyes on the car in his rearview mirror. Sure enough, Declan turns into the salon's parking lot.

I swallow the lump in my throat. "No. Keep driving."

Rome nods once and reaches over the console, lacing his fingers between mine. "Whatever you want, tré-sur."

Rome sets a modest pace as he drives through the city, so we don't get pulled over.

Midtown at night is quiet and pretty, even though the

wintry wind is threatening snow tonight. The businesses are closed, but their signs of bigotry are loud, hurting me with their stalwart declarations of *"Humans Only"*.

I tried. For all my effort, I changed nothing and no one.

Except for myself, I guess. I am changed, perhaps irreparably.

We make it to the border, both holding our breath as we cross over the city limits and cruise the countryside, leaving our families and the whole of Mayfield behind.

Love the book?
Leave a review!
Otherwise, Orlando dies.

27

THE SCANDALOUS CITY PREVIEW

Enjoy a Free Preview of *The Scandalous City*, Book Five in the Last Deadblood Series

Valentino Cabin

Rome hasn't made me talk about the reason why I decided tonight was the perfect evening to run far away from the city we have fought so hard to save.

I know Rome is holding himself back from prying. My boyfriend is grateful that I took him up on the offer he made earlier this week to run away and not look back, no matter how badly the city falls to ruin in our absence.

Instead of asking me to name and define the multitude of demons on my shoulder, Rome turns on an opera I love in hopes it will quiet my silent angst. He holds my hand while the music soothes us both.

Again, it's the perfect thing to do. I'm not sure how he found out my favorite opera and had it ready to play, but at this point, I am starting to expect Rome always knows the best thing to do in any situation.

A memory dawns on me of Daddy Valentino belting out in his best vibrato a song from this very opera. I remember how weightless I was in his arm, perched happily while he gestured in sweeping movements with his free hand.

My favorite opera was a gift from Daddy Valentino, which is most likely how Rome knows it, as well.

We are the same, which is a truth I have known for quite some time.

Every now and then, Rome's thumb traces over my fingers, reminding me that I am only as alone as I would like to be, and never more than that. His presence calms me beyond any serenity I could achieve on my own.

We drive past the city until the buildings become fewer and farther between. Soon enough, we are the only people on the road for miles. The rows of towering trees on either side lead the way to a quiet peacefulness I wasn't sure existed a couple hours earlier.

Snow falls in a light dusting, giving me the illusion that we will be covered from all who seek to destroy us. The only greenery left lurks beneath pine trees that dot the side of the freeway. Even they are well hidden by the snow as it accumulates the longer we drive. They will keep our location a secret. They won't tell the world that we are gone, and Mayfield is on its own.

I could ask Rome where he is taking me, but I don't care. I don't want to know because then I would exist somewhere. I want to exist nowhere, floating so my misery cannot pin me down. So I sit in silence for two hours, grateful for the quiet that doesn't make me stand when I can barely breathe without heartache.

The lull of the opera helps. The soprano taps into emotions I have a hard time expressing. And I certainly couldn't do so with this sort of eloquence and beauty.

The trees thicken the longer we drive, choking out capitalism with a valiant effort. I've not spent much time in the woods, other than Orlando hiding me away in his cabin not too long ago. We were never a family that went camping together. In fact, other than our recent catastrophic family dinner, the four of us don't spend much time as a group if we can help it.

Too much baggage to poke at, I guess.

We used to go on family vacations with the Valentinos,

but that was before the split between our families, back when I was a child with optimism left to spare.

I expect the same non-vacation life of the Valentino family now that us Kennedys have. So when a large, rustic cabin finally comes into view, my mouth falls open.

"Is this yours?" I ask, breaking the silence for the first time.

Rome cuts his gaze to me. "It is. I bought it when my father passed. I used a human ID to purchase it."

My head whips toward him. "You have a human ID?"

Rome manages half a smile. "Of course I do. I wouldn't be able to own property outside of the West End if I didn't. And people would be able to easily track me down whenever I want to disappear." He winks at me. "Can't have that."

I point to the long two-story cabin. "Is this where you went when we…"

Rome nods, his jaw tightening. "When I was an idiot and left you because we were mid-mating and I freaked out like a child? Yes, it is. So if I ever leave again, this is where I'll be. You and Orlando are the only two people who know about this place."

I gape at the property, appreciating it anew. "You're full of surprises, Mister Valentino."

"That's why you love me, Madam Deadblood. Every now and then when things get too intense and I can't see which way I should go, I drive out here and bury it all in the woods until I understand myself a little better."

I turn my chin to marvel at him. "I love it."

Rome parks the car in the attached garage. In true Valentino fashion, even their interpretation of rustic comes with all the trappings of a life lived lavishly. There are sconces of what look like animal bone lighting the inside of the spotless garage.

I am in a daze when Rome grabs our suitcases and my purse, and then takes my hand to help me out of the car.

We did it. We got out of the city.

Rome kisses the back of my hand, looking at me through thick, black lashes. "Welcome to your new home, Mrs. Valentino."

My heart spasms inside my chest. It's a joke, clearly—him giving me his last name. Vampires can't legally marry humans. Plus, we only just got back together. Thoughts of permanence are a leap, since we don't have the best track record.

I incline my head to him. "Mister Kennedy."

If I have to give up my last name for this little joke, then so does he.

Rome barks out a laugh that surprises us both. I didn't think anything would be funny ever again, but he is always the man who challenges my worldview and takes me to the next level.

When we step inside, Rome leaves me only to turn on

the breakers so the lights can show me a side of this man I never knew existed.

This is Rome's private sanctuary. It's the home he shares with no one because it is his. Every other part of him he has sacrificed for the redemption of Mayfield, but this place remains his alone.

The decor is rustic chic, because a Valentino never settles. Everything looks straight out of a catalog for someone trying to imitate a hunter's paradise.

I am grateful there aren't any animal heads hung on the walls, though that seems to be the only thing missing.

The rich polished oak baseboards run the lengths of the maroon walls in the main living area. There's a lush cream-colored rug in front of the fireplace, begging me to spread out on it and sleep for weeks. The sconces on the walls are the same polished animal bone. There is a lamp on the wooden end table with a bespoke oil lantern shape that mimics the curve of a woman's hip.

The chandelier is a gargantuan thing that demands respect. The antlers are clearly fake, but they jut out three feet across the ceiling on either side of the soft light. The buttery leather couch looks like something a king of old would lounge around on, with golden studs on the armrests.

"Rome," I whisper, still in awe that this place exists, and that somehow, I have landed myself here.

"Do you like it?"

It's not until he speaks that I catch the note of insecurity in his tone. I turn to stare up into the bright blue of his eyes. "I love it here."

His shoulders relax back into the perpetually unruffled state I have come to expect from him. Despite the late hour, his black fitted slacks aren't wrinkled and his white dress shirt with the cuffs rolled is uncreased. His thick obsidian hair is gorgeous, and perfectly in place. "I'm glad to hear it. Whenever things get too intense with work or your family, you tell me, and I'll take you here. It's a good space for clearing your mind and starting fresh."

Rome leads me through the living room and up the steps to the two bedrooms and office, which all reflect the same warm, contemporary rustic polish that the living room holds.

Of course Rome's vacation home has an office. He is exactly like me, and never learned how to properly unplug from his duty or ambition.

When we reach the first bedroom, he places my purse atop the plush comforter. The bedding is pure white, standing out like a luxury hotel selling point in the middle of the woods. The walls are wooden and unpainted, giving the feel that Rome has created a small paradise smack in the middle of nature.

We truly are hidden away.

My fingers twine through his when it finally dawns on me that my problems are literally miles away. Hours away.

I don't have to confront any of it here. This place has a quiet peacefulness to it that the city has no interest in providing for me.

I angle my chin up at Rome, who is watching me process this place with a silent concern, no doubt worried that I might bolt at any second.

I can't help it that I'm a runner. I ran from my family when they treated me like an acquaintance, which is how we ended up here. Yet standing next to Rome, I have no desire to flee the scene. Rome is unruffled, even though it is the middle of the night. His trim figure doesn't slouch, though I know he must be tired. His angular jaw gives nothing away, watching me but keeping his words tucked inside.

I let go of Rome's hand and walk further into the room, my fingers feathering over the fluffy comforter.

I mean to tell him "thank you," but when my lips part, the unvarnished truth spills out, polluting the woodsy aroma in the air. "My father is dying."

I blanch at my confession, regretting bringing those words into this haven.

Rome startles, taking a step back. I guess neither of us expected I would lay it all out this easily and so soon.

Rome's nostrils flare. "What? Was he shot? We have to go back, then. I'll get Elias to a hospital." Rome is already marching for the hallway, a man on a mission.

"It's cancer, not a bullet," I call after him. "He's refusing treatment. The doctor says he'll be dead in the next few weeks. Chemo would have given him a few months, but he's not interested."

Rome turns to face me, his mouth dropped as he grips the doorjamb. Emotions I am too distressed to process myself flood his features, reminding me that I should be able to react to horrors normally, rather than finding a way to run from them.

Still, I can't feel any of it. I am mired in shock and rage.

And fear. Beneath the anger, there is a scared little girl, being confronted with the fact that her tower of a father is in fact fragile.

Of all the things the sheriff has been to me, fragile has never been one of them.

CONTINUE THE SERIES AND READ *THE SCANDALOUS CITY* today!

USA Today bestselling author Mary E. Twomey lives in Michigan with her three adorable children. She enjoys reading, writing, vegetarian cooking, and telling her children fantastic stories about wombats.

While she loves writing fantasy, dystopian, and paranormal tales for her readers, Mary also writes romance under the name Tuesday Embers, and cozy mysteries under the name Molly Maple.

Visit her online at www.maryetwomey.com, and sign up for her newsletter, so you never miss a new release.